I0640177

Bad Cop 2

Sa'id Salaam

Published by Black Ink Publications, 2020.

Email: **blackinkpublications1@gmail.com**

Facebook: Free Sa'id Salaam and/or Black Ink Publications Like Page

Cover design and layout by: Sunny Giovonni

Edited by: Tisha Andrews

SYNOPSIS

Megan begins a new life without her father in it. Even worse is that her mother is in it. The two constantly bump heads as she comes of age. Fate moves the family out of their comfortable home into a strange new land.

Megan struggles to learn her new surroundings as well as herself. Most of those lessons come from her favorite pastime, people watching. Through it all she keeps her eyes firmly on the prize of a shiny badge and gun.

BAD COP 2
A Novel By
Sa'id Salaam

Chapter 1

I guess I watched a little too much TV because I had totally unrealistic view of the legal system. In my mind Jax was going to get sentenced to death and electrocuted later that day. Hmp, I'm the only one who was in shock.

"This is some real bullshit! Grade A, 100%, pure bullshit!" Marinetti pronounced. His pale face turned beet red with rage yet his lip quivered as if he might cry.

"I'm not happy about it either, but the DA signed off on it. Says would have had a hard time convicting Jax on murder charges. Plus, Ruiz is a much bigger fish," the assistant district attorney explained. What he didn't explain was how good shit rolls uphill, just like bad shit rolls down. Bagging Ruiz would get the district attorney a judgeship which meant he would move up to his spot.

"Bigger feather in his cap you mean!" the cop practically spat and stormed out of the court room. He couldn't bear to sit there and watch the cop killing cop get a slap on his wrist.

"Excuse you!" Michelle fussed when Marinetti almost bumped into her baby bump on her way in. She was now showing but still didn't speak on being pregnant. He mumbled an apology in transit and kept it moving. She lifted her head and continued inside.

Megan felt silly in the matching mini skirt and pumps her mother forced her to wear. The woman loved to show off so much her vanity extended to her daughter. She found a boutique with a junior thot section and bought inappropriate outfits for her daughter. She'd already burned through over a hundred grand of the insurance money. Rohan tried to set his family up for life if he lost his, but at the rate she was spending it wouldn't last a year.

"That's for the defendant's family," bailiff explained when Michelle attempted to sit on the wrong side of the court room. It was populated by Jax's pretty mother, girlfriend and daughter.

"Oh, OK," she said stealing glances at the women in his life. All were pretty, well dressed and decorated with diamond and gold etcetera. She stuck her lip out comparing the girlfriend to herself. She claimed victory over the much younger woman but only because she had been drinking already that morning. She gave the woman's pretty daughter the win over her own since Megan was on the chubby side of life.

"All rise!" a bailiff announced when the door to the judge's chamber came open. The court had to rise and fall when the judge came out from his chambers and took his perch. A pompous tradition he'll have to answer for when he stands before the Judge of judges, King of kings.

"What's first?" the judge asked even though he already knew. His clerk did too but still made a show of flipping through files. The court room was clear of reporters as well as other defendants because of the deal to come. A deal so sweet they didn't want anyone else to witness it.

"State verses Jackson," she announced. On cue the bailiff went to side door to retrieve the prisoner.

"Hey Poppi!" Michelle called out when Jax appeared in his Rikers Island green garbs. He ignored the cat call and smiled over at his mother, woman and daughter in order of importance. Her daughter looked up at her as if she was crazy. Michelle got a half nod from Jax as he took a seat at the table with his lawyer. He knew all about her claims to be pregnant as well as her love for him through the letters she wrote daily.

"I understand a plea was reached in this matter?" the judge asked knowing one had been since he approved it. He too would have liked to give the cop killer a lethal injection but this was an election year and he had political aspirations of his own.

"It has your honor," the prosecutor agreed and stood. "The state agrees to fifteen years for possession of narcotics in exchange for his co-operation in other matters."

"Defendant?" his honor said to Jax's attorney who stood. Jax stood, too, to accept the plea.

Megan felt her breath stop when she looked at the man who murdered her father. A flashback of him naked came but she shook her head and dismissed it. She froze when he turned his head and made direct eye contact with her. It was only a split second but seemed like an eternity. The world began to spin again once he turned back to the judge.

"Guilty your honor," Jax offered. He was ready to get back to the jail so he could smoke some weed and eat some free world food. Junior kept his word and made sure his time would be as cushy as possible. He had one corrections officer bringing weed and alcohol. Another made sure he didn't have to eat the slop served in the chow hall and more lady cop serving hot vagina a couple times a week.

"Bye babes! I'll wait for you!" Michelle called out as he was escorted back through the door. Jax didn't look her way but his mother and baby mother both turned with frowns. She made a tacit declaration by placing a hand on her belly before speaking. "What? Y'all got a problem?"

Megan shrank in her place a little since she knew her mother was drinking and smoking that morning. She swerved a few times on the drive in to the city. It wasn't the first time her inebriated mother had embarrassed her and it certainly would not be the last.

*****

"We going to see your grandma," Michelle announced when they were back in the vehicle. She needed Reese to see her outfit and new purse since part of showing off is showing to other people. Still her mind was consumed with the sizzle, razzle and dazzle of the laced blunts she'd become reacquainted with. Even the little junky in her belly was expecting a hit.

"OK," Megan nodded in agreement. She'd done her homework and was ready for grandmother. "Can I have my allowance?"

"Yeah, remind me to go by the bank later too," she said knowing she was down to a couple hundred dollars in cash. She parted with a twenty once they reached the projects. Megan already knew the drill and headed up to Dianne's apartment while her mother made her way over to her friends.

"It's me, grandmother!" Megan called as she knocked on the metal door.

"Hello sweetheart!" the old lady sang as she opened the door. She let out a rich burp fueled by malt liquor and giggled, "excuse me."

"That's OK. Let's play Tonk. I have my allowance!" she replied. Dianne should have seen she so too eager to lose.

"Let me get my purse," the lady said intending to fill it up. Meanwhile her daughter arrived at Reese's intending to get high.

Reese had a mouthful of dick when her friend knocked on the door. The woman knew opportunity knocks so she tightened her grip on the shaft and stroked a little harder. The man in her mouth began to moan and soon she had a mouthful of cum.

"Whew!" she said a millisecond after gulping down the babies who would never be. Her guest tucked his deflating dick away and stood. He dug into his pocket to pay the fare of an afternoon blow job. The door knocked again instead of replying.

"Thanks yo." he said parting with a couple dime sacks of crack. He was ready to leave when she opened the door.

"Just who I was looking for!" Michelle cheered, making both Reese and Lil Wop wonder which one she was talking to. She narrowed it down by digging into her purse and coming out with money. "Let me get an eight ball."

Reese discreetly tucked the rocks she just sucked him off for away since her friend was buying. She would smoke as much of hers up and save hers for later.

"Hard?" he asked to clarify. Both he and Reese rejoiced when she nodded in agreement. He looked down at her belly as he pulled an eight ball out of his pocket. He'd sold plenty of drugs to plenty of pregnant woman so it didn't faze him in the least. They exchanged dope for dollars and he left them alone.

"That's a bad ass outfit! Let's smoke a Woolie," Reese cheered genuinely. She was being a rare sincere since it was a bad outfit and she did want to smoke a Woolie blunt.

"Got weed?" Michelle asked since she didn't. She had plenty at home where she was smoking crack laced joints and blunts on a daily basis since she started a couple months back.

"A little," she replied and reached under her sofa. She fumbled between the two and came up with the smaller envelope half full of brown weed. Michele turned her nose up at the regular weed since she always spent extra on the exotic weed of the day. Reese felt some kind of way about the slight, but held her tongue since the woman had three and a half grams of South Bronx's finest crack cocaine.

"Let me see that," she said when Reese filled the shell of a Dutch Master cigar with the brown weed. She laced it with roughly with crushed rocks and handed it back. Reese's eyes went wide at the amount of dope she put in it. Not that she was complaining, her money just wasn't long enough to smoke like that.

"OK then, baller," she cheered and licked the blunt. She sealed it with saliva and semen since she just sucked the teen off. Her hands shook in excitement as she lit the blunt.

Michelle watched and inhaled with her as she took a long sizzling pull from the blunt. She felt her stomach churn and got slightly turned on by the sights, sound and smell of the Woolie.

"Two tokes and pass!" she reminded when Reese took another pull. She sucked with all her might and held the smoke deep in her soul as she passed it. Sips of air kept it in and pushed it down so she could extract as much of the drugs from the smoke as possible.

Now it was Reese's turn to watch as she smoked. She felt jealous watching her take a long pull despite still holding smoke in her lungs. It wasn't until she felt dizzy did she blow the smoke out and take a breath.

An eerie silence settled in the room except the sizzle of one of the most dangerous drugs on the planet and the din of the projects beyond the window. There was nothing to be said until Reese took a final pull on the roach.

"That was dope!" Michelle said ironically since it was the dope she was cheering about. Night fell by the time the scant weed supply was diminished.

"We still got a gram or so?"

"And no more weed or blunts. We could call Lil Wop, but then we still gotta go to the store and buy blunts," Reese said. After carefully laying out the problem she offered a solution.

"Camille left a shooter over here. We could, use that?"

"I, um, guess," Michelle reluctantly agreed. It would be a first for her but not Reese since the crack pipe was hers, not Camille's. Camille didn't even fuck with her anymore after she fucked her teenaged son and his father, so she couldn't prove it wasn't.

Michelle and Reese smoked the rest of the dope through the pipe and opened the next chapter in their lives.

Chapter 2

"Wake up, lucky," Dianne called into her daughter's old bedroom to wake her granddaughter. She dubbed the child 'lucky' after she cleaned her out last night. It wasn't luck that the smart girl researched Tonk, Black Jack and several varieties of poker.

"Yes, grandmother," the obedient child said, sitting up and rubbing her eyes. Megan was dog tired from being up all night. She had stayed up long after her grandmother got drunk and retired. She watched the late night activity in the courtyard including her mother making several trips to the bench where Lil Wop and company slung their dope.

Michelle could have purchased some weed to switch back to Woolies but that's not how that works. You don't get a stripe and give it back. No, she would have to reach rock bottom first. Then, look up and make the decision to reform or die. She and Reese were polishing off the last of the dope that the last of her cash purchased while her daughter polished off bacon, eggs and biscuits from a can.

"Thank you, grandmother," the polite child offered once her plate was cleaned. She took it a step further by clearing the table and washing the dishes.

"Thank you, baby girl," Dianne sang gratefully. She noticed her daughter's growing belly and drug problem, even though Michelle didn't admit to either. All she could do was hope the woman wouldn't have to go through what she did to get clean. A wave of anguish swept over her knowing that would have to.

Michelle shook her head as her friend pushed and pulled on her straight shooter trying to recover one last hit from the residue. She let her have that since she was headed to the bank later. After a few hours sleep that is since she'd been up for over 24 hours now. She decided to hit Lil Wop up for credit now and pay him when she came back into the city.

"Well," Michelle said and stood. She wobbled, fell back on the sofa and tried again.

"Shit, I'm fucked up! Let me take my ass home."

"You ain't tryna get nothing else?" Reese pleaded like a full-fledged junky. The full night of smoking verses the occasional session pushed her to the point of no return. She was all in from that night on. Dicks would get sucked, shit would get stolen, whatever it took to keep her pipe full.

"Nah, that was all the cash I had. I'll prolly hit the bank later and pull a few grand," she bragged. "Check, let me hold on to this?"

"This? Um..." she said not wanting to part with her pipe. She still had the two dimes she got out of the dealer's dick and planned to smoke them after a nap of her own.

"Here," she said pulling ones, and coins totaling eight bucks. "Just buy her another one."

"Who?" Reese asked since she forgot blaming the crack pipe on Camille. The glass tubes turned into straight shooters only cost a buck plus another buck worth of steel wool. The extra two, three dollar hits she could get with the left over six bucks was enough to seal the deal.

"Bet."

"Should leave little mama with her grandmother," Michelle mused as she made her way to the door. She shook her head 'no' knowing the girl would have a meal cooked when she woke up. She let out a sigh and headed over to her mom's to collect her child.

She hoped Lil Wop would have been out so she could credit some dope 'til later. He was upstairs in a semi coma from smoking blunts and slinging crack all night. The day shift of dealers was on the bench instead. She didn't know any of them but they all knew her from Lil Wop always bragging about how good she was spending. The direct results of her spending could be seen in his upgraded wardrobe.

"Where Wop?" she asked hoping someone would volunteer to go get him.

"Sleep!" two of the four announced in unison hoping to make the sale. One left it alone so not to have a problem with Wop but the other was about his dough.

"What you tryna cop?" he dared, looking at his friends to see who didn't like it. There was a standing rule not to fuck with others steady customers but dude was sleep after all.

"An eight ball but I gotta hit the bank and bring the money back," she explained. Both her child and Reese watched the interaction curiously from windows in opposite sides of the courtyard.

"Thought you ain't have no money! See, I hate bitches like you. I got yo ass!" Reese fumed like the woman owed her more than the hundreds of dollars worth of drugs she smoked with her the night before.

"Let's go home mommy," Megan pleaded out loud. The smart girl knew she was buying drugs and knew how their lives were changing because of it. The child practically had to raise herself for the last few months.

"I'm good ma," he declined, poking his bottom lip out for emphasis. He was too young and green to understand the value of credit. His was a cash and carry world so he turned his head and tuned her out.

"Little bastard," she mumbled as she turned away and walked to the building. She was inside when she heard someone rush in behind. The project veteran spun and put her fist up in case it was some bullshit.

"Chill ma!" one of the teens from their bench said, raising his hands in surrender. "I'm saying tho, I might can fuck with you on some credit."

"Cool, let me get an ounce and..."she began but his shaking head interrupted her request.

"I ain't even balling like that ma. I can front you like, ten dimes," he said leaving himself enough to re-up with. The younger dealers bought packages they could flip for a quick double up.

"OK, it'll have to do. I'll be back out here later and bring you your hundred dollars," she agreed and extended her empty palm. It would stay empty a moment longer while he laid out the rest of his terms.

"I'ma need a buck fiddy back on the credit," he began, then paused. When her head began to nod in agreement with the first half he laid out the second part. "And I'ma need some dome."

"Nigga you tryna tax me on the interest and, want your dick sucked!" she exclaimed in astonishment. He thought he went too far and opened his mouth to back down. Luckily for him, she spoke first. "Come on with it."

"Bet!" he cheered and went for his zipper. He tricked enough with the local junkies to know to hold off giving her dope until he got his rocks off. A female crack head is as fast as an adult cheetah with crack in hand. If one runs off there's no catching it.

"What's your name, boy?" she asked as she squatted. A necessary formality since she was about to let him put his dick in her mouth.

"Grip," he said as she helped free his penis from the huge baggy jeans the teens favored. His nickname wasn't as cool as his big brothers but Wop being the oldest he got to be called Lil Wop after their dad.

"Mm," Michelle moaned as he grew hard and thick in her mouth. She was oddly turned on while giving him a blow job since she hadn't had sex since Jax was arrested months back. Her designer, maternity panties went from moist to wet while she worked.

"Dang, ma!" Grip announced as she sucked him from zero to sixty in a minute. He went stiff and sent a spurt of semen towards her tonsils. "Hey!"

"Hey, my ass," she giggled as she pushed his dick away. He quickly grabbed it at stroked himself finished. "Now come on with it. I'll be back in a few hours."

He twisted his lips as he parted with his dope and put his dick away. She took her prize and rushed up the pissy stairs to her mother's floor.

"Hey. mommy, can we go home?" Megan pleaded as she ran over and hugged her. She knew the drugs that were changing both of their lives came from here so she wanted to retreat to the safety of the suburbs.

"Yeah baby,"'she replied sympathetically from the remorse. The salty aftertaste of the come was all that prevented her from planting a kiss on her forehead.

"Hey, Michelle," Dianne greeted somewhat sadly. She recognized the effects of a hard night of smoking hard on her child and felt helpless. She knew how vicious she could be too and opted to hold her tongue.

"Hey, ma. We bout to bounce. I gotta..." she replied and turned towards the door to escape her knowing gaze. She was almost out in the hall when her mother called out.

"Oh, yeah. Can I hold a few bucks?" she asked leaving out that her granddaughter beat her out of her money.

"I ain't got no cash on me," she replied leaving out that she gave it all to the local dope boy. "I got you when I come back."

"OK, sweetie," Dianne sang and waved. Michelle and Megan waved back before taking a deep breath to hit the stairs.

*****

"Are you OK, mommy?" Megan wondered as her mother swerved through the parking lot. She nearly hit a parked car and clipped a junky on the way out.

"I'm good yo," she shot back and focused to make it true. Easier said than done since she nodded at the red light.

"It's green, mommy," Megan called out when the truck didn't budge.

"What!" she snapped before the car behind her laid on its horn. Megan was relieved that someone came along to deflect her ire. "Mother fucker I see the damn light! With yo bitch ass!"

Megan always got a kick out of her mother's ghetto girl tirades. She could mimic her to the T but only in private, in front of the mirror. Her mother was just one of the colorful characters she had in her impersonation repertoire. She even did a mean Beyoncé even though she was round like Precious.

Megan was watching the world go by on the expressway as they sped towards Long Island. She didn't notice they were actually speeding until a Nassau County police car flipped its lights on and slid behind her. Michelle showed no reaction to the police car and kept driving. Not because she was being defiant or anything but because she was sound asleep.

"Um, mommy. The police want you to pull over," the girl said cautiously. Her mother woke up and strained her face. She almost seemed surprised that she was behind the wheel.

"Shit!" she fussed and swerved again. She corrected herself and put her blinkers on to pull over. "Say you aren't feeling well and I'm trying to get you home."

"OK, mommy," the girl agreed. Once they were pulled over the cop got out and approached the car. Megan carefully studied his every move since she planned to make those same moves when she became a police officer.

"License and registration," the no nonsense officer demanded. He saw she was clearly sleeping when he was behind her and seeing one child in the vehicle and another in her belly perturbed him. Pissed him off actually after all of the nasty fatalities he'd seen on duty.

"What's the problem, officer?" Michelle sang sweetly and made the problem worse.

"Have you been drinking, ma'am?" he demanded already decided that she had. The faint smell of alcohol on her breath and red eyes made him ask although it was obvious. "Please step out of the vehicle, ma'am."

"Out, why? I'm pregnant," she said, searching for reasons not to comply. The officer radioed for back up and repeated himself. "Oh OK!"

"You too please, young lady," he said turning on the charm as he turned to Megan. She appreciated it since that's how she intended to deal with children when she was a cop.

"Yes, sir," she replied courteously, like her dad trained her to do with dealing with adults. He directed them both to his car to have a seat while he waited for back up. She was going to jail if, or when she failed the field sobriety test so someone would have to transport the child.

"Mind if I search the vehicle?" he asked once they were seated in the back seat.

"I don't care what you do! I'll be calling my lawyer to report..." Michelle began her next rant until he closed the door. He'd received permission to search so he went to do just that. Another car pulled up by the time he reached the truck.

"What we got?" a fellow cop asked as he pulled up and got out. He glared at the two back seat passengers to hazard a guess but came up short.

"DUI, at the very least," he replied and began his search. He started with the purse on the center console and struck gold. Crack actually, when he discovered the small baggies of dope along with the straight shooter. "Jackpot! Call Child Protective Services."

The other cop made the call to get a social worker on scene before they would make the arrest. Megan could tell from their faces that something was wrong. Michelle had gone back to sleep and was snoring softly beside her. She let her sleep until the first cop came to retrieve her.

"Ma'am?" he asked opening the door. He had to call a couple more times before waking her. "Step out so I can have a word with you please."

Megan watched a third car pull up on the scene and guessed correctly that things had gone from bad to worse. The middle aged white lady with sensible shoes had social worker written all over her.

"Can we go now?" Michelle groaned as the cop escorted her away from the car.

"Ma'am, we found drugs in your vehicle," he began so he could read her the Miranda rights and place her under arrest.

"They not mine! Must be my daughter's. She's been acting strange lately," she explained to his astonishment. That changed everything as far as he was concerned.

"OK. Let's sit you in the other car." he offered taking her and placing her in the back seat of the other squad car. "Vince, call Pilgrim State Hospital. This bitch is crazy!"

Chapter 3

"Hello, sweetie. My name is Mrs. Stanfield. What's yours?" the social worker sang softly when the cop opened the door. Megan twisted her lips dubiously at the woman's feeble attempt to distract her from her mother being arrested. "How old are you?"

"Is my mom under arrest?" she turned to the cop and asked. He turned to the social worker for help as Michelle was driven away. She wasn't cuffed since she was pregnant but she was still in the back seat. "For the drugs?"

"She going to get some help," he assured her once again looking to Mrs. Stanfield for help.

"That's right, miss?" she asked once again hoping for a name. Megan twisted her lips and analyzed her for a moment before declaring her safe.

"My name is Megan. I'm ten. No, eleven," she said remembering her birthday that passed almost unnoticed. Michelle slept that day until videos went off like any other day. She only remembered when she came out and saw the girl had baked herself a birthday cake. Michelle got a piece and retired to her room and partied like it was her birthday.

"Well Megan, do you know your address?" the woman asked.

"I'm eleven," she replied twisting her chubby face. "Of course I know my address."

"Is your dad home? Do you have a dad?" she asked causing Megan to look at the cop wondering if the woman was serious. He rolled his eyes in tacit support but kept quiet.

"My dad is dead. I can stay home by myself though," she said leaving off just how much time home alone she spends. As time went on she was home alone even when her mother was home.

"I'm sure you can but do you have a grandparent you can spend a few nights with?" Mrs. Stanfield asked. She would hate to have to check this sheltered child into the group home. The wild girls there would eat her alive as soon as she got there.

Megan gave up Dianne's info as well as her own. She got in the car with the social worker and rode out to her own house to pack a bag. From what the cops told her it could be awhile before the mother returned.

"Are you sure you live here?" the woman asked when she pulled into the driveway. Megan pulled her keys out in response and got out.

The woman had a right to be surprised since most of these calls came from Wyandanch or Brentwood. Not middle class enclaves like this. She was slightly jealous of the neatly furnished, and clean home. She took the liberty of looking around while Megan packed a bag of clothes.

"Oh my!" she reeled when she entered Michelle's disheveled room. It reeked of stale menthol, weed, beer and crack smoke, soaked into the carpet and drapes. She took pictures of the scene for later use when it came time to determine if the child could go back into the home or not. A pretty vibrator on the night stand had caught her attention and cocked her head curiously.

"What's that?" Megan asked as she came in behind her and saw her inspecting the device.

"What? Nothing!" she said tossing it back on the clutter of the night stand. It would have ended up in her purse if she hadn't shown up. She turned and rushed the girl out to the car for the ride back out to the city.

*****

"Where the hell are you taking me! Who do you think..." Michelle fussed when the police first pulled away from the scene. A deep yawn cut her off and batted her eyes. She was far too sleepy to raise hell and decided to get a nap.

Much to the officer's relief since he wasn't in the mood to be yelled at for the whole ride out to the state run mental hospital. An hour later they arrived and it was him yelling at her to wake up. She didn't budge so the cop copped a free feel. He groped one titty, then the next one then patted the mound in her panties.

"Ugh!" he grimaced feeling the wet panties. Not wet because she was turned on but because she had peed herself.

"Wake up! Fucking retard!" he fumed and pulled her out of his car by her arm.

"Hey! What the fuck is wrong with you!" Michelle fussed at being snatched from both her sleep and the back seat. She twisted her lips as she looked around trying to figure out where she was. The ivy covered, hundred-year-old buildings had institution written all over it but it didn't register. "Where are we?"

"Pilgrim State!" he shot back as two intake orderlies came to collect her. He had some paper work to fill out but first things first. "Where's the bath room? I need to wash my hands!"

Michelle fussed and cussed but didn't resist the large orderlies. She knew she was going inside one way or the other and opted for the easy way over the harder one.

"Name?" the intake clerk asked with an exclamation point rather than question mark.

"Why am I here? Fuck they bring me here for?" Michelle shot back. She looked around at patients shuffling and shaking from the effects of their meds.

"For whatever reason the officers felt you were a danger to yourself and children. Do you want to hurt yourself? Do you want to hurt anyone?" the woman asked in the calm manner of a mental health professional.

"Bitch, I'ma hurt you if you don't let me out of here!" she snapped. That was the wrong answer and the orderlies swooped in and restrained her. She cussed and fussed some more as she was secured in a straight jacket. A nurse slid a needle in her arm and everything went black.

*****

"Oh my. Oh my. Oh... my!" was all Dianne could say when Mrs. Stanfield filled her in on the day's events. Megan sat quietly nodding in agreement to the reports of the drug use.

"Well at least she can get some help," she offered softly. "Well, I have to drive back to Long Island. Here's my number and for Nassau County courts."

"But a mental hospital?" Dianne pleaded again. She recalled some of the crazy shit she did when she was strung out and nodded. She would have agreed wholeheartedly had she known the woman tried to put the drugs on her child.

"Would you like to walk me to my car?" Mrs. Stanfield sang to Megan when she stood to leave. She was eager to make out the housing projects safely.

"No," she replied honestly but that's not the answer her grandmother would accept.

"Girl, walk Mrs. Stanfield to her car," she fussed. Dianne stood and shook her hand and let her out.

"You'll be just fine. Your mom will too once she gets some help and rest," she comforted as Megan led her down the hall. They hit the pissy steps and out through the lobby.

The group of girls Megan watched from the window were coming from the bodega with quarter waters and chips when they emerged from the building. Megan was too naive to understand not to stare at people so she did.

"Who that bitch, Na-Na? Why she looking at you?" the sidekicks hyped like sidekicks do.

"I'on know! She must got beef?" the leader declared. She lifted her arms daring Megan to reply.

"Thanks for the ride!" Megan blurted and took off into the building. The hood rats took off after her since she ran. Her weight and lack of activity made her slow. Luckily she had a big enough head start to make it to the apartment.

"What's wrong with you?" Dianne demanded when she burst back into the apartment.

"Huh? Nothing!" she said, locking the multiple locks behind her.

"Un uh, we don't do no running around her!" Dianne announced and pried her granddaughter away from the door. She unlocked the locks and peered down the hall. It was completely empty to Megan's relief. "I was 'bout to say..."

There was nothing to say since the girls made their way out to the courtyard. Megan watched and listened as they high fived and bragged about running the girl off. Soon the subject turned to boys so she tuned in to listen, mocking them to amuse herself.

*****

It took a few days for Michelle and her mother to convince doctors that she really wasn't crazy. They kept referring back to her blaming the drugs on her child because that was some crazy shit. Not being crazy came at a cost since she now had to face criminal charges for the drugs. A collect call ensured her mother would be present to arrange her bail.

"Why don't you have a car?" Megan asked when she and her grandmother set off on the long journey to Long Island without a car.

"Cuz I'm from the Bronx!" she shot back as if that explained it. It did since the majority of city dwellers traveled by public transportation. In fact, a car was sometimes more trouble than it was worth.

Megan twisted her lips at the answer as they stepped from the building. If they were driving or riding they would have exited the front towards the parking lot. Public transportation meant cutting through the court yard to catch the bus.

"There she go! And got her lips twisted like you did her something," a girl warned, pointing at Megan.

"She tried you!" another one cosigned like the drunk uncle who keeps squirting lighter fluid on the grill.

"You got a problem with me!" Na-Na challenged, throwing her arms wide.

"Who you talking to, Nashanda?" Dianne dared. She grew up in these same projects with her mother and grandmother.

"Not you, Miss Dianne. That girl keep trying me!"

"Me?" Megan asked incredulously. "What I do?"

"You must want a one?" her grandma challenged.

"Hell yeah!" the child shot back since the days of respecting elders was long gone.

"A'ight. That's a bet! Wait 'til we get back!" Dianne shot back. Her grandchild was a big girl so she assumed she could hold her own.

"I'ma be right here!" Na-Na said as if she would ever be somewhere else. There was a very good possibility she would spend the rest of her life right there on the park bench. Sure she might take time off to give birth a few times but it was pretty much as far as she was going.

"But grandmother, I don't want to fight that girl," Megan pleaded as they marched away.

"Too late now! You 'should'na been messing with her then," she scolded.

"But, I didn't! Besides... I don't even know how to fight!" she insisted.

"Well, you better learn."

Chapter 4

"Wait, she said what?" the judge grimaced as the officer testified. He wiggled a finger in his ear to clear whatever was obstructing his hearing because he would not believe what he just heard.

"She said the drugs belonged to her child. Her ten-year-old," he repeated making Megan's eyes go wide with shock. She wanted to stand up and clear her name as well as correct her age but held her tongue. Even Dianne was taken aback by that one and she pulled some pretty outlandish stunts during her tenure as a crack head.

"Wow," the judge marveled, scratching his head. He'd thought he heard it all after 30 years on the bench but this was definitely a new one. A doctor from Pilgrim State was next to testify and didn't make it any better for Michelle. She wasn't particularly worried though since she had enough money in the bank to cover whatever her bond would be. Then she could shoot uptown and cop some rocks. A week sober was too much on her. She got high to escape reality but now sober, she had to deal with it head on. And what an ugly reality it was being pregnant by your husband's killer. Large doses of drugs and alcohol were needed to numb that truth.

"Well our initial diagnosis was paranoid schizophrenia, but later discovered she was just high," the doctor nodded along with himself.

"Pregnant and high?" he interrupted for clarification. Judges are supposed to remain impartial but this pregnant woman had crack in her system with a baby. Not to mention, crack in her car with a child, and blamed it on the child.

"High as a kite your honor! Her blood work showed an incredible amount of cocaine and marijuana in her system. Oh, and she was drunk. And weed, there was a lot of weed in her system as well," the doctor added. He enjoyed watching the judge turn red in anger since Michelle pissed him off too by asking him to bring her drugs.

"This bitch is crazy," the judge muttered to himself. The court reporter heard and debated whether or not to transcribe it. She shook head 'no' and left it off the record.

"Your honor we request bond on her own signature," the court appointed lawyer spoke up for the first time. It was standard practice to request for standard drug possession. If you're white it's a good chance you would get it, black though, not so much. Still a bond would be granted for users. Usually ten thousand, which she could stand.

"The state request no bond. She should be held for the welfare of her unborn child!" the assistant district attorney shouted over to her colleague instead of the judge. The two women argued back and forth while the judge shifted his head back and forth, watching the verbal volley.

"Eh um, excuse me, but I believe I have some say in the matter?" his honor interrupted.

"I'm ordering she's held without bond for the welfare of her child. Then, a ten thousand dollar, cash bond once she gives birth."

The pounding of the gavel ended the case but not the discussion. The two adversaries bantered back and forth as Michelle processed what she'd just heard. She was so focused on her plans to get high she missed most of the narrative.

"Wait, so I can't go home?" she asked as the deputy came to remove her. She would be taken to the county jail where sadly enough they had a maternity ward full of pregnant addicts.

"Thank God," Dianne sighed. She'd seen enough crack babies to rejoice at the decision.

"What's going on grandmother?" Megan pleaded as her mother was rushed away, raising hell every step of the way. She was still loyal to what should be instead of what was.

"She going to get help. Come on, let's go back to the city," she said and led her out of the court room.

****

Dianne tried to distract her distraught granddaughter by talking about each and everyone they passed. Megan was slightly embarrassed by her antics but found herself cracking up at her wise cracks. They were having so much fun they both forgot about the play date waiting back at the projects. Until they got back to the projects that is.

"There she go!" a girl called out when Dianne and Megan walked towards the projects from the bus stop. Several girls were posted up like sentries at every entrance waiting for them to return. There was always plenty to see and do in the projects but a good girl fight gets top billing every time.

"I see her!" Na-Na said smearing Vaseline on her face and removing her earrings.

"I think that girl wants to fight me?" Megan warned her grandmother of the activity. People stopped doing what they were doing and formed a crowd to watch.

"You think? She does, and you're going fight her!" Dianne demanded and picked up the pace. When they reached the pack she laid out the rules. There aren't any rules in a street fight except, "Don't jump in! This is a one on one!"

"But, grandmother, I..." Megan pleaded once more until her grandmother shoved her forward. She had no choice now but to try to reason with Na-Na. "Listen, I..."

Reasoning never had any place in a street fight either and Megan found that out in a hurry. Na-Na attacked so fast Megan didn't stand a chance. The ghetto girl slapped, punched and scratched her while she stood there. Her arms rotated like a windmill as her friends cheered her on.

"Beat that bitch ass! Punch! Kick!" came the instructions from ringside like a prize fight.

"Fight back! Duck! Block, something!" Dianne pleaded as the girl got pummeled.

"Five-0!" someone yelled, instantly hit the pause button in the projects. The dealers stopped dealing, the smokers stopped smoking and the fight came to a sudden halt.

"OK, OK. Break it up," Officer Johnson sang. The older cop had a grandfatherly tone and vibe which got him grandfatherly respect. "What are you girls fighting over? You again, Na-Na? What, a boy?"

"She was talking mess!" Na-Na declared pointing at a confused Megan.

"Me? I, didn't, say anything!" she huffed and puffed, bruised and lumped.

"Just some little girl stuff," Dianne sang flirtatiously. He flashed a smile at what they once shared. Not a real relationship since he had a wife and children at home. But lunchtime quickies, and secret rendezvous until her drug problems consumed her world like a California wild fire.

"So, this is over right?" the officer asked looking back and forth between the combatants. The dazed look on Megan's told him this was on Na-Na so he focused on her. "Na-Na, is this over?"

"As long as she ain't talking no more shit! I mean mess!" she fussed, correcting her French when he scowled. She could barely speak English so she had no business speaking French.

"OK then. You girls shake hands," he insisted and stepped back so they could.

Megan flinched again, getting giggles when Na-Na extended a hand. Dianne shook her head as her granddaughter shook one of the hands that just whooped her ass.

"Let's go," she huffed and pulled the girl towards the building. "Why didn't you tell me you didn't know how to fight!"

"I did," Megan insisted as they headed back up to the apartment.

*****

"Are you sure?" Dianne asked again. She just couldn't believe her nerdy grandchild didn't want to go to school. Her mother still had three months before giving birth and making bond. "You can't just sit in the window."

"Yes I can because I'm not going to school here," she said making, 'here' sound like a curse.

"Bougie ass," her grandmother mumbled and walked off. That was fine by Megan who turned back to the window to watch the goings on down below.

She bucked on traditional school in favor of learning about the streets from her bird's eye view. It was Streets 101 as she slowly put pieces together.

It didn't take long to realize that most of the boys sold drugs to the local addicts. What amazed her is they all used drugs themselves. They smoked weed, drank beer and popped an occasional pill while selling hard cocaine to fellow residents and visitors.

A good number of the older project dwellers worked nine to five jobs. Most of the younger ones sold drugs or had some other hustle. Oddly it was almost like the suburbs multiplied by a million.

Time passed as quickly as life in the projects moved. A New York minute, as it's called. Megan was still in that window when they got the call they'd waited three months for.

"Get dressed big head!" Dianne fussed for a third time when the first two request went unheard. Instead the fight outside the window had her full attention. She realized she got off lightly as she watched Na-Na beat a teenaged girl into the fetal position. That's when her cronies ran up and began kicking and stomping. There was a lesson learned in that too; don't hit the ground. No matter what, stay on your feet.

"Where we going?" Megan asked mimicking the odd way the project dwellers spoke. She often amused herself and grandmother with her impersonations.

"No time for games, Megan. Your mother is having her baby!" she fussed. She wished she was catching a bus over to Lincoln hospital on 149th street instead of a bus, a train and another bus out to Long Island.

"Ooh, Ooh! OK, OK!" she cheered, bounced and clapped as she put her sneakers and coat on. "I hope I have a little brother! No, a sister!"

"Gonna be one or the other, that's for sure. Now let's ride!" Dianne quipped and led the way outside. She let out a little sigh and shook her head when her granddaughter lowered her head in the presence of the bully. She knew her baby wasn't built like that but it still didn't sit well with her. Her daughter Michelle fought every chick in the projects at one time or another when she grew up here. Still she knew the two were nothing alike, even if Megan did spring from her womb.

Megan used lowering her head as a defense mechanism anytime she was outside. Na-Na would glare at her, daring her to make eye contact so she could pick a fight. Dianne knew it wouldn't last forever and the bully would be back to bullying her baby. She would no longer accept the sign of submission and push the issue. Hopefully her daughter had her act together enough to take her home. She had a newborn to raise, too, so that would leave no room to party.

Two hours later they were still an hour away since buses and trains run on their schedules not the riders. Finally, they reached the Nassau county jail where Michelle was still being held. They arrived shortly after the baby made its debut into the world.

"Hello, mama!" Dianne cheered when she saw the bundle of joy on her chest and exhaustion on her face.

"Hi, mommy," Megan greeted unsurely. She just never knew which one of her mothers she was getting on any given day. The stress she felt instantly upon seeing her made her realize just how stress free she was without her around.

"Hey, you guys!" Michelle sang happily, basking in the afterglow of child birth. "Megan come here and meet your brother."

"I was hoping for a little brother!" she squealed and quickly crossed the room. She pulled the baby blanket from his head to get a look. "What's his name? Let's name him after daddy!"

"I did. His name is Jax Jackson," she said proudly. She had no way of knowing her daughter assumed this was her father's child.

"Huh? Daddy's name is, was, Rohan. Rohan Robinson," she declared. It took a second for it to sink in and break her heart.

"Oh no," Dianne moaned as she did the math. Her daughter got knocked up a month after her husband got knocked off. She knew enough about the case to recognize the name.

"Fuck you shaking yo' head for, yo?" the other Michelle snapped as she made her appearance, causing Megan to take a step back out of her reach. Another look at the infant spread a scowl on her face since she knew the name as well. She backed away vowing to have nothing to do with the child ever.

"Nothing, baby. He's my grandson and I'm going to take him home until you get out," her mother said calmly, hoping to soothe her.

"Well, I already wrote a check to the bonds company so they gonna get me out in the morning," Michelle said jubilantly. Dianne recognized the glow in her eyes and knew she planned to get high first chance she got. Her drug habit had been in hibernation for months and was ready to escape its cave and roar like a grizzly bear.

"You sure you don't want to rest a few days?" Dianne pleaded.

"In jail? Bitch...no. Fuck no! Take my son home and I'll be there tomorrow night," she said, thrusting the newborn towards her.

Dianne had already agreed to take custody of the child so paperwork was signed and she was allowed to leave. She and Megan traveled in silence on the bus, train and a bus again. Both dealt with the reality of the baby as well as Michelle's return. Neither was pleased about either.

Chapter 5

Bastard. n. 1 person born of parents not married to each other. 2 unpleasant or despicable person. I chose 2 to describe the boy child my mother gave birth to. He was not my brother, just the bastard child of the man who killed my father. I vowed then to have nothing to do with him.

"You wanna hold him?" Dianne asked when she saw Megan staring at the baby from across the room. The words were already out of her mouth by the time she registered the look on her face.

"No!" she shouted despite the risk of what came with disrespecting elders. She wanted nothing to do with the child of the man who killed her father and said as much. "He killed my daddy!"

"No, baby. Your little brother didn't do anything. He's an innocent baby," she pleaded.

"Now your mom will be home today and she's going to need your help."

"Can you come home with us? Please?" Megan moaned breaking her grandmother's heart. It was yet another sign that the child was being abused.

"Sure. Your mom will appreciate the help," she nodded with herself, trying to convince herself. The look in Michelle's eye told her the woman longed to get back into the streets. Someone was going to have to look after these children. The look in her granddaughter's eye told her she would let the infant starve if left up to her.

*****

"Let me up out this bitch!" Michelle barked as she was processed out of the jail. She took the papers with her court date and tossed them in the trash as soon as she got them.

"See you when you get back," the jail worker laughed at her throwing the paperwork away. She'd seen many do that when they get out and saw them again when they come back. Missing court date is a surefire way of coming back to jail. Next time there would be no bail since they skipped bail in the first place.

"My shit don't even fit!" Michelle grumbled as she put back on the maternity clothes she was arrested in months back. "That's cool cuz a bitch got gwap! I'm 'bout to hit the bank and hit the mall!"

Michelle finished processing out of the jail and did just that. A branch of her bank was a block away so she hoofed it over to make a withdrawal. She took her standard ten grand out to get back on her feet. First order of business was getting off her feet and back into her vehicle. She took a taxi over to the impound lot to claim her vehicle.

"Run me my shit, yo," Michelle demanded slinging her paperwork on the counter. The woman pressed her lips together tightly and entered the information into the computer. A gentle smile spread on her face at the results.

"Seven thousand, one hundred and twenty-five dollars please," the clerk requested when she tallied the total.

"What! Bitch I already bought and paid for my damn truck! Fuck you mean, seven thousand!" she fumed.

"Seventy-five dollars a day, times 95 days. Seven thousand, one hundred twenty-five dollars," she repeated politely despite being called a bitch. She'd be a bitch for seventy-five hundred dollars.

"Like a bitch can't stand it!" Michelle bragged and produced a stack of racks. She made a big production out of counting out the money and shoving it through the hole in the bullet proof partition. "Now bring me my shit!"

"Yes ma'am," she sang happily since they were seven grand richer. She radioed to the rear and the truck was brought around front.

"Y'all niggers could at least washed my shit!" she fussed at the sight of her dusty vehicle. She cussed and fussed as she got in and drove away.

Michelle wanted nothing more than to go see her babies. Not just her newborn but even Megan as well. First she needed to get out of the oversized maternity clothes. Couldn't let Reese or anyone else see her down bad. She turned towards Suffolk County with the best of intentions.

*****

"Grass needs cutting," Michelle griped when she pulled into her driveway and saw her overgrown yard. She still had good intentions when she opened her door and entered. "Home sweet home!"

Michelle intended to call her mom to check on her kids but after three months of showers and child birth, she was ready for a bath. She adjusted the temperature and fixed a drink while the tub filled. Meanwhile she stripped out of the ill fitting clothes and into her robe.

"Oh yeah!" she cheered at the weed in her panty draw. A good joint while soaking in the tub was just what the doctor ordered. She reeled at the sight of the crack under the weed and slammed the drawer. "Just a joint. I ain't fucking with that shit. Un uh, not today."

Michelle lifted her chin in defiance and pulled the drawer back open. She selected a matching bra and panty set as well as the weed and closed it back. Despite the fact that the crack was trying to explain itself. Trying to reason how she deserved a hit after her ordeal. She wouldn't have to go crazy, just lace up a joint and relax. Nothing serious, just...

"OK, damn!" she relented and retrieved the crack. She dumped a little into the joint and twisted it up. Once she eased into the water she sipped her drink and lit her Woolie joint. That's how it started once again.

"Un, un, un," Michelle grunted and gyrated along with the videos on TV. She'd missed quite a few new releases in the three months she was gone but got caught up in a hurry. She debated on whether or not to smoke another laced joint and decided it would probably be best. The ringing phone interrupted her plans when she took the call.

"Um, hey baby," Dianne said softly. She knew to verbally tread light-ly so not to set her volatile daughter off. She also knew from experience that a crack head just needs the slightest reason or cause to justify get-ting high. She hoped to get her with her baby to curb what she knew Michelle would be dealing with. The whispers of the devil that get so loud they consume a soul.

"Sup ma?" she questioned, ready to snap to counteract the guilt of getting high.

"Yeah um, so I called the jail to check on you and they said you was already gone?" she eased over the egg shells.

"And? So, what you 'sposed to be checking on me or something? I'm a grown ass woman and I..." she snapped.

"No, baby. I was about to go to the A and P! I just wanted to know what you wanted me to cook you for your coming home dinner," Di-anne pleaded to placate.

"Oh! OK, cuz... yeah," she chuckled and calmed down. "Yeah I had to stop by my house and, yeah so un huh. I'm on my way. You making fish and spaghetti?"

"If that's what you want, baby," she agreed even if it meant she really did have to go to the supermarket. Her meager food stamps were stretched to the limit trying to keep her chubby grandchild full. At least Michelle could now help out.

"OK, I'll see you in a bit," she said and hung up. She turned to the crack and informed it "You gonna have to wait. I need to go see my ba-by."

*****

"OK, I know you in yo' feelings but I need you to watch him while I go to the store," Dianne demanded. She saw Megan's face begin to twist and tossed, "unless you wanna run over to the A and P?"

"No!" Megan quickly snapped at the thought of going out without grandma's wing to hide under. She was in the window and knew Na-Na and her crew were posted up. Despite it being a cold New York day they reported to the park bench as if on payroll. In a sad twist they inherited the bench from their mothers. One of the girls was actually conceived on that same bench on a warm summer night.

"OK then. Watch him so I can get something for dinner. Your mom wants fish and spaghetti," she explained. That was enough to get the stubborn girl to relent.

"OK. I'll watch him," she agreed literally. Meaning she would look at him but do no more. No bottles, changing or baby talk. Just, watch. Watch him cry, wet himself or even choke, but wouldn't touch or talk to it.

She didn't even do that because as soon as her grandmother left she popped back into the window to see what she could see. This was her last chance since her mother was coming to take her home. She learned lessons in the three months that wouldn't register until later in life. Some that would help her when she became a police officer someday. She'd witnessed enough criminal activity to spot it before it even happened.

"So?" Megan quipped at little Jax when he began to whimper and cry. She knew from watching her grandmother that he was either wet or hungry but neither mattered to her. She agreed to watch him and would do no more. By the time Dianne returned he was bawling out of control.

"Megan!" Dianne reeled in disbelief when she walked in and saw the girl literally watching the baby scream his little lungs out. His screams were so loud some couldn't be heard by human ears.

"I watched him," she shrugged and turned back to the window just in time for an argument to escalate to a fist fight.

"Nuh uh. Go brown the meat since you wouldn't change your brother!" her grandmother fussed as she tended to her grandson. "Black hearted little ass letting him just cry."

"Awe man," she moaned at missing the fight and complied. She didn't just learn about the streets over the last three months. Her grandmother schooled her on the domestic side of life. She could now cook almost anything, most from scratch.

Dianne barked orders from the living room while she rocked the baby and watched the TV. Soon the spaghetti was done and the fish was frying. Perfect timing when Michelle used her key to enter the apartment.

"Uh oh! Smells like you did your thing!" Michelle cheered as she entered and smelled the food. Her initial high had worn off and she was starving. She was grateful she didn't smoke the heavily laced blunt in her purse. Despite arguing with it the whole way into their city.

"There is your mommy," Dianne cooed to the baby as his mother approached. She watched for any signs of drug use as she handed the infant over but saw none. She smiled proudly as the mother took her baby and sat beside her.

"Where's Megan? Outside?" she asked since Megan stayed in the kitchen to listen for which one of her mothers showed up. She didn't know what bipolar was but knew what it looked like first hand.

"Tuh!" Dianne huffed at the thought of the timid girl outside. "She's in the kitchen."

"Hello, mommy," Megan greeted as she came around the cinder block wall into the living room.

"Hey, pretty girl," she sang, making her daughter blush and giggle at the compliment. The good mother was here so she rushed over and hugged her neck making sure to avoid the bastard baby.

"I'm hungry, ma," Michelle announced once the loving was done. "Can you fix me a plate?"

"Sure, baby," Dianne eagerly agreed and went to do just that. She fixed one for Megan as well and sat both on the small dinette table. "I'll hold him while you guys eat."

"Thanks, ma," she said as she and her daughter took a seat at the table and dug in. "Dang ma! What you did different?"

"What's wrong? It's not good?" she reeled judging by her daughter's screwed up face.

"Good? This shit is delicious!" she corrected and shoveled more into her mouth. She saw Megan beaming in pride and asked, "You made this?"

"She sure did!" Dianne cheered proudly since she taught her. Sure the girl adlibbed a little in the spice rack but she still taught her. The family had a touching moment over dinner and desert. Life was good but it couldn't last.

"I'm about to go check out Reese for a minute. I'll be back," Michelle announced, suckling all the air out of the room. Both Megan and her grandmother wanted to protest or plead for her not to go but neither wanted the other Michelle to pop up. They helplessly watched her walked from the apartment. Megan rushed to the window and watched her cross the courtyard. A single tear escaped when she stopped by the bench occupied by the local dope boys. She flipped out the window unable to watch the transaction.

Chapter 6

"Hey!" Grip announced in protest and pointed as Michelle approached. He remembered she owed a debt but the details were blurred by three months' time and strong weed.

"I didn't forget you, little man, I got bagged. My ass been sitting up in Nassau County since that day!" she explained when she reached the crew of dealers.

"They don't play out there!" a dope boy cosigned with his eyes going wide for exclamation points. Plenty of city kids venture out to Long Island in search of bigger profits and end up in prison.

"Word," Grip agreed since his big brother Lil Wop was sitting on Rikers Island for drug charges himself after getting caught in a sweep of the projects.

Officer Johnson either turns a blind eye to the dealers or runs them off. As long as they didn't disrespect him by dealing in his face. It was a different story when the narcotics squad conducted their drug sweeps and clean house. Anyone caught up in it was going to jail. Lil Wop and his little crew were spared and waiting on court dates to get their slap on the wrist. The judicial system played a cat and mouse game with these teens. Slapping their wrist and spanking their bottoms with probation and skid bids of six months here and there. Then once their record is bad enough they can hide them up north for a decade or two.

"So what I owe you?" she asked even though she knew. She figured he wouldn't remember but was ready to settle up either way and spend a little as well.

"Shit... like, what fifty?" he guessed. He did remember that good blow job and wanted a repeat. "Plus some dome."

"Ain't no dome popping off my dude but here...Let me get an eight ball too," she said handing him enough to cover both.

Reese strained her eyes trying to count the money along with him from her window. She was grateful to see her old friend back and copping rocks since she had graduated to smoking crack daily. She made a sick prayer that the woman would bring her some of whatever she was buying. Her prayers weren't answered because only God can answer prayers and that's not one He would. Michelle still turned towards her building and began walking. Reese ducked out the window so not to appear as if stalking.

"Who?" Reese called out quite believably when Michelle tapped on her door. Michelle twisted her lips instead of replying and the door came open anyway. "Oh, hey girl! I ain't know you was in the city! Where you been?" she sang as she let the woman in. She tried to remain calm but knew the woman had dope. Her stomach churned in anticipation of her next hit.

"Long story girl! I...where yo' shit at?" she shrieked at the blank space her entertainment center use to live.

"Girl, I got robbed! Took me two years to pay that shit off and niggas run off with my shit. Oh, you had the baby!" she said noticing her stomach was gone. The truth of the matter was she robbed herself to buy more drugs.

"Yeah, a boy," Michelle said leaving out the word yesterday. Instead she produced the weed and crack and ordered her friend to, "Roll up."

*****

"Can we go home?" Megan asked when her mother returned late the next afternoon. After three months in the projects she was more than ready to return to her own home. Her own room, school and life.

"I'll go out there with you guys to help out with the baby," Dianne offered. She watched the courtyard herself last night from her bedroom window and knew her child was back on the drugs. She was back and forth from the building and bench until the wee hours of the morning.

"Um, I gotta..." she replied searching for an excuse. She only came to retrieve her purse so she could go to the bank to get more cash to smoke more drugs. Somewhere around midnight they gave up on the foreplay of Woolies and fucked with the pipe raw dog.

"Baby..." Dianne said woefully and set her off like a detonator.

"Baby what? I said I got some business to handle and you sweating me! I gotta get out of here cuz I can't with you people!" she said. She grabbed what she came for and tore off out of the apartment. Reese was waiting in the pissy lobby to take the ride out to the Island.

"Shoot, we should just hit Spanish Harlem and buy some weight instead of letting them nickel and dime niggas nickel and dime us with eight balls," she suggested as if it was both of their money.

"That's what's up! Yo, 'member when we met dude from Jersey?" Michelle laughed at the decades old memory.

"Oh yeah! Nigga tryna cop weight and we made his ass wait!" Reese cackled at the come up. The man knew Spanish Harlem had the dope but didn't know who to get it from. Reese and Michelle convinced him that they did. They took his ten thousand dollars and walked into one of the walkup tenement buildings and walked out the back door and left him sitting there. They laughed about that and more of the foul stuff from the past but the worst was yet to come.

Michelle barely made it to her local branch before closing time and withdrew her usual ten thousand dollars. The teller frowned up curiously when she noticed the same transaction from a day earlier.

"Is everything OK, Mrs. Robinson?" she had to ask. For all she knew she was being held hostage and paying ransom.

"I will be when you give me my money," she shot back curtly. She was ready to get high and didn't have time for twenty questions.

"Excuse me," she quipped and completed the transaction while mentally calculating how many more withdrawals of this amount she could make. It wouldn't be many and she wouldn't have to deal with the nasty woman anymore.

Michelle drove above the speed limit all the way back to the city. She was beat from giving birth followed by staying up all night getting high. The New York native expertly navigated the city streets until she reached Harlem. It had been over a decade since she last copped from the area but nothing had changed. Nothing will ever change because there's too much money to be made.

"Sup, mama. What chu tryna cop?" a young Dominican man asked when she pulled up and got out.

"Couple of ounces," she decided for starters. They stepped into the lobby to conduct the buy. The purchase wasn't large enough to be invited upstairs so the runner ran and got the dope.

"Nice!" she exclaimed at the large lumps of glistening coke. She rushed back to her truck where Reese anxiously awaited. "Yo! Check this shit out mama! It's raw so we gone have to cook it."

"We going back to the projects?" Reese frowned as she pulled away from the curb.

"We could go to my house?" Michelle asked herself and pondered. Her house certainly was more comfortable than the projects. "Yeah, let's go to my house. We can hit the liquor store and get some..."

"Moet!" Reese suggested since it wasn't her money. They would have to split a 40 ounce malt liquor had she been buying. A final stop for baking soda and supplies to cook and smoke dope. Even the baby food she bought to use the jar to cook coke in weren't enough to make her think of her baby.

****

"My mother's not coming back is she?" Megan asked when Michelle failed to show up the next day. It had been a full 24 hours since she left and they hadn't spotted her last night. Both kept vigil on the courtyard but Michelle or Reese weren't spotted.

"Probably not," Dianne heard herself admit aloud. She wanted to clean it up and sound positive but wasn't in the mood. The reality was that her daughter just left her newborn baby to go get high. She stuck her chest out and accepted that reality and everything that came along with it. "You're going to school!"

"Here? With Na-Na?" Megan shrieked. As bad as she was ready to go back the thought of attending school with these wild project children scared her. Especially Na-Na. She managed to avoid her by ducking and dodging but being a coward didn't sit well with her either.

"Yes, here. You ain't no better than no one else!" her grandmother snapped little harder than intended. It was another truth so again she left it be instead of trying to clean it up.

"OK, grandmother," she pouted. It would be the obedient child's only protest. It was settled and she was going to school in the Bronx. She gave in on that but wasn't budging when it came to the baby.

"Well, hold your brother while I..." Dianne began but Megan got up and walked away before she could finish. Dianne could only shake her head because she sure couldn't blame her. She decided not to push her on the matter since she saw right then she was as stubborn as her mother. The only question now was would it work for or against her.

Days passed by and Michelle was still a no show, no call. Ironically both Megan and her grandmother got use to life without her. The baby never met her and wouldn't miss her. At the speed she was going he may not ever meet her.

Chapter 7

"Well, baby," Dianne sighed after she finished registering her grand-child into the local public school. Meagan's eyes were wide with shock from the loud boisterous children. This was another planet from the safe suburbs she was used to. They passed by several fights just making it to the office.

"I'm fine, grandmother," she insisted even though she didn't quite believe it herself. She did love her grandmother though and didn't want her to worry. Besides, this was still a school and she loved to learn. She would hold her head high and focus on her future in spite of those without one.

"OK, baby," she relented even though she didn't believe it either. These kids would eat her alive but, she probably wouldn't die. If it didn't kill her it could only make her stronger. The girl needed to toughen up anyway because life is tough. Megan was escorted to her class by staff and introduced to her teacher Mrs. Helms.

"Hello, Megan. If you're here to learn sit there," she said pointing to one of the empty chairs in the front of the room. "If not, get in where you fit in."

"Here is fine," she said after following her finger to the rear of the class. She saw Na-Na glaring back and ducked her head. A roar of laughter followed her getting punked out, but she came to learn. Mrs. Helms nodded in approval at her decision. As a teacher she was always delighted with kids who actually came to learn.

Megan learned more than the reading, writing and arithmetic. She was already light years ahead of her classmates even though many, like Na-Na were older than her. That gave her plenty of time to study her favorite subject, people.

Girls, boys, teachers and staff were all analyzed and locked in. She would take their personality quirks home to study along with her regu-lar homework.

Na-Na kept a vigil on the new girl in hopes she would get out of line but Megan wouldn't take the bait. That meant she had to up the ante, because that's what bullies do.

*****

"Give me your pizza, fat girl!" Na-Na demanded from standing over Megan in lunch hall. She had successfully avoided the girl for almost two months but time was up.

"My... pizza?" Megan asked in total confusion. The lunch food wasn't very good except tater tots and pizza. Despite Dianne's best efforts she wasn't able to feed the girl like she was used to. Megan ate breakfast and lunch in the cafeteria to augment what she couldn't eat at home.

"No bitch, my pizza!" she said and reached for it with her friends egging her on. The pack of junior hood rats cheered when she reached for the girl's food.

"No!" Megan shouted and grabbed the girl's scrawny wrist. Na-Na grunted in pain and a look of fear spread over her face like a rash when she felt the strength of the chubby girl's grip.

"Get off me!" she screamed and tugged. She was totally helpless because she couldn't get free until Megan let go. Na-Na stepped back rubbing her sore wrist. Na-Na really didn't want to mess with her anymore but the 'oohs and aahs' from the crowd insisted otherwise.

"Oh hell no! Beat dat bitch ass!" her sidekick demanded, starting a chant.

"Bitch, wait 'til we get back to the projects. I got you. Just wait!" Na-Na ranted and raved because she had to, not because she wanted to. It sounded good but she hoped the scary girl would duck out as soon as the bell rang and rush home while she and her friends laughed and joked their way home.

"You not getting my pizza though," Megan said to herself when the mob moved on. She took a big satisfying bite of her pizza as Na-Na robbed another girl for her lunch.

She had a date with danger after school but her mother had problems of her own.

****

"Whew!" Michelle cheered after she and Reese polished off brunch. They didn't eat much but ordered take out when they did. All the local eateries loved them since they ate good and tipped better. "That shit was good!"

"Girl that was good!" Reese agreed. "You don't be cooking? I see you got all these accessories and shit."

"Yeah, my husband used to buy everything that came on the TV." she quipped then went silent at his memory. He was such a good man that death was better than life with her. Her children were a mere afterthought in her life now. She reminisced while Reese added up all the accessories and etceteras like crack heads do. If push came to shove she would smoke this entire kitchen.

"I needed that sleep. What day is it? Saturday?" Reese asked scratching her head. They both slept for a full day after a two day crack binge. The two went hard but every now and again, their bodies claimed its right over them and forced them to sleep. This latest crack nap happened to coincide with them smoking the last of their drugs. Running out of crack and money was a good time to take a break. They would sleep for a couple days before hitting the bank and going hard once more.

"I think so?" Michelle replied since they partied like everyday was a Saturday. "Ooh, I hope not cuz we gotta hit the bank?"

They were both relieved to see it was only Tuesday. They both showered and changed into fresh outfits from one of their frequent shopping sprees. Life was shopping, smoking and the occasional meals and sleep. That meant a trip to the bank, then uptown to cop. They were now running through an ounce a day. Balling out of control.

"Girl, what's that noise?" Reese asked when Michelle pulled out of the subdivision. She turned the radio down a little so she could hear it too.

"I'on know," she frowned curiously upon hearing the engine complaining from lack of oil and maintenance. It hadn't had a tune up or oil change since Rohan died.

Michelle repaired the annoying sound by turning the radio back up. She began to dance in her seat to the latest jam. Reese joined in too and they partied all the way to the bank.

The same teller was having a rough morning after a rough night of arguing with her boyfriend. She perked up instantly when she saw Michelle enter the bank. This was the day she had been waiting for. It was her and she planned to enjoy it. She breached protocol and waved her directly to her counter.

"Baller shit," Michelle bragged to the grumbling patrons she bypassed in the line. She matched the woman's smile when she reached her and slid the withdrawal slip across the counter. "The usual."

"Yeah, no I'm sorry but you don't have sufficient funds to cover this request," she barely got out through her wide smile. A happy giggle escaped, despite her best efforts not to laugh in her face. She threw her hand over her mouth to stop it but the look on the woman's face was priceless.

"Excuse me? Fuck you mean I ain't got sufficient funds? Bitch, I got hundreds of thousands in this bitch!" she barked, lifting her head and voice in a big show. The teller had a little show of her own and slid a receipt across the counter. "What is this?"

"Your balance, ma'am," she proudly announced. She'd been waiting for this day and it finally arrived. It was about to be cut short by the curious manager making her way over to the commotion.

"Bitch, how the fuck I only got 13 dollars left in my account? My husband left me hundreds of thousands of dollars! And a house! And a car! And a..."

"Mrs. Robinson, step over to my office so I can assist you," he said and turned away so she would follow. The angry clicking of heels behind him told him she was right behind him.

"Have a seat."

"I don't want no damn seat! I want my money!" she insisted putting a hand on her hip.

"I have your account transactions printed out. Please, sit," he offered once more. Michelle sucked her teeth and complied as he laid the papers in front of her.

"Hmp," she huffed as she flipped through pages and pages of counter withdrawals, ATM withdrawals, and debit card purchases. Her head shook slowly as it added up to her tricking off all her money. That didn't mean she was just going to accept it though. "I think that teller been stealing from my account!"

"No ma'am. Your account spending was flagged and monitored. She actually inquired about it with you," he reminded.

"Oh, um OK. Well, I still need cash. Can I take some money against my house? It's paid for you know?" she said desperately grasping at straws.

"I know it is since we held the mortgage," he replied spreading a smile on her face. His next words erased it just as quickly. "Except the house is in your daughter's name."

"Oh, OK. No problem, I'll go get her and bring her back so..." she decided and stood to do just that. Michelle abandoned her children in favor of drugs but would go straight to the Bronx and pick her up to get this money.

"Has she turned 18 yet?" he asked knowing that she hadn't. The house couldn't be borrowed against, sold or anything until Megan was of age to do it herself. They spent the next half hour going over scenarios that would allow her to leave with some cash. She would toss them up and he would shoot them down like at a skeet range.

"Awe hell!" Reese moaned when she saw Michelle's angry strides out of the bank. She knew this day would one day come and was ready for it. The end of the cash was just a bump in the road as far as she was concerned. "What's wrong, mama?"

"They bugging, yo!" she said clutching her 13 dollars tightly in her fist. She through the truck in reverse and slammed on the gas.

"Chill, yo!" Reese warned when she almost hit another car. "Yo, we still got racks of gear with the tags on them. We can take that shit back and get cash. Not to mention all that fly shit you got in yo' house. Bitch, we still straight!"

It was pure crack head logic but Michelle was a crack head and it sounded logical. Her husband had a jewelry box full of watches and trinkets just sitting. They had bags and bags full of unworn clothing from their shopping sprees. It wasn't over just yet but the free fall to rock bottom had officially began.

Chapter 8

"Ooh, girl. We gotta go so we can catch big girl!" Na-Na's second in command, Yvonne, announced when the bell rang. Megan quickly stood and rushed out just like she did every day. That allowed her miss all the fights and drama of the day. The other girls usually played around after school, taking an hour to make the ten minute walk back to the projects.

"That bitch don't want it with me!" Na-Na shot back. It sounded tough but she could still feel the grip the girl had on her wrist. She knew she only got loose when Megan allowed her to.

"Come on!" Yvonne insisted and led the charge. Megan moved quick for a big girl and made it to the projects before they caught up.

"There goes your sister," Dianne cheered when her granddaughter entered the courtyard. She had a habit of keeping a vigil with the baby for her to return from school. She also held hopes her daughter would return from the dark side. The smile on her face dissipated seeing the mob of girls running up behind her. "Oh, boy."

"Talk that shit now!" Na-Na shouted as she ran up and pushed Megan from the rear. She hoped the girl would take off running so she wouldn't have to fight. Megan had other ideas and turned around to discuss them.

"Look, I..." she began, once again trying to reason. Once again she got her ass kicked for talking instead of fighting.

Na-Na couldn't fight in the classical sense; she was just wild. She rotated her arms like a windmill delivering slaps and punches while Megan stood there. Once again it was Officer Johnson to the rescue as he came over to break it up.

"OK, OK! That's enough!" he said once again pulling Na-Na off her ass. "You two again! Still fighting over that boy?"

"She was talking mess!" Na-Na explained huffing and puffing from the lopsided fight.

"She tried to take my pizza and I said no!" Megan shot back in her own defense. Even Dianne was shocked to hear her defending herself for once.

"Well it's over now, so everyone go home!" the cop insisted. No one actually went home but they did disperse. "Except you. Come here."

"Yes officer, sir," Megan replied in awe and reverence of the uniform and badge. Both she intended to have one day for herself.

"Here. You come down here on Wednesday and Friday nights," he said handing her a card while looking towards Dianne for approval. She batted her eyes coyly and nodded.

"P.A.L?" Megan asked reading the large letters on the card. They were explained in smaller letters right underneath so she kept on reading, "Police Athletic League. What this do?"

"Lots of stuff, but it's gonna teach you how to fight. Make sure she's at the gym tomorrow night," he said turning from grandchild to grandmother.

"OK," Dianne said submissively. They began walking back to the apartment when she whispered, "Come by later."

"I will," he whispered back. Both needed to learn how to whisper because Megan heard every word.

"Here, take him while I cook," Dianne tried once again and once again got shot down.

"I'll cook," Megan said defiantly and walked into the kitchen. The baby was several months old and she still had yet to touch, talk or even look at him. Dianne understood at first but this was too much. She had to accept that her sweet little granddaughter had a cold heart.

****

Megan only stayed up watching the courtyard on weekends now that she had to go to school. She made sure to keep her same routine and went to bed earlier enough to beat the mob to class.

Baby Jax slept in a crib in Dianne's room since his half-sister wouldn't have anything to do with 'it' as she called him. Never by his name, or 'the baby', just 'it'. Strange noises from the front woke Megan in the middle of the night. A glance out the window showed the usual suspects doing the usual suspect shit in the courtyard. The noise was coming from the inside so she crept forward to investigate. She played cop as she eased out of her bedroom. Grandma's door was open so she peeped inside through the crack. All she saw was the empty bed and the bastard baby sleeping in 'its' crib.

"Sss, mm," came from the front so she dropped low and slithered down the hallway. She stopped short at the bend to the living room and listened. She knew those sounds well but leaned in for a look anyway.

"Mmhm," Officer Johnson agreed as he dug grandma out good and slow. He buried his big dick inside of her and just grinded.

"Sss," Dianne repeated. The woman was in her late fifties but her vagina still worked and she knew how to work it. She wiggled and squeezed her way to a couple of orgasms before he began to moan and groan as his approached.

Megan covered her mouth at the old couple copulating but kept watching. Watched as the cop bit down on a throw pillow to stifle his outburst when he burst inside her grandmother. Grandma squeezed and wiggled some more making him thrash around in ecstasy.

"Shit, that's good!" he exclaimed in a whisper as he pulled out of her.

"Good as it used to be?" she asked with a washcloth to wash his and hers come off his dick and balls.

"Better," he replied and stood. He pulled his uniform back on and prepared to leave. Not without breaking bread first and dug into his pocket.

"Thank you, baby," she purred at the fifty dollars. Megan saw enough and eased back down the hall. She slid back into bed and went to sleep with what she saw on her mind.

*****

"Rise and shine sleepy head!" Dianne sang as she stuck her head into Megan's door.

"I'm up," she replied cocking her head curiously. Her grandmother was practically floating around jubilantly as she prepared breakfast. It reminded her of her own mother after hearing her and her father having sex. Michelle would be in a great mood the next morning too. She was still too young to connect the dots and shrugged it off in favor of the big breakfast.

Megan side eyed the baby as her grandmother fed him across the table. He was putting on, doing his cute baby routine but she wasn't impressed.

Fuck that baby she thought just like she heard Lil Wop saying the other night when one of the project chicks told him he had a son.

"Thank you, grandmother," Megan said appreciatively when her plate was cleared of bacon, eggs, biscuits and hash browns. She would have washed their dishes before school if Dianne hadn't stopped her.

"I got them. Here baby," she said handing her some money.

"What's this for?" Megan asked looking at the fifty-dollar bill in her hand.

"For you. Buy yourself something you want," she stressed. She was stretched to the limit trying to take care of her grandkids without any help but was tired of seeing the girl do without.

"Just be careful, OK?"

"Yes, grandmother. Thank you, grandmother," she sang and breezed out of the apartment. Megan was careful and didn't let anyone see her spending any money. She'd seen enough kids like herself like her get robbed by Na-Na and her crew.

*****

"What now?" Michelle asked once they returned all the new clothes and smoked the refund. She knew what was next but wanted it to be Reese's idea. This way she could pass the blame of the fuck shit to her.

"Shit... All them watches and shit ain't doing shit but sitting in a damn box," she replied. The box was short a watch and a ring she swiped and hid for later use. Reese stashed quite a bit of valuables for when the inevitable arrived and the well ran dry. It would be each crack head for themselves at that point.

"I was gonna save them for Jax when he come home but... " Michelle started then stopped when the baby came to mind. She shook her head tersely to remove his little face and moved on. "I know a spot out east."

Michelle was a junky but knew enough to dispose of the high priced items at a high priced store out on the Island. Had she went to any of the spots in the city that dealt with crack heads she would have gotten crack head prices.

Even still the twenty thousand dollars worth of jewelry only netted six thousand at the second hand jewelry store.

"That's plenty!" Reese cheered and took note of the address. It was plenty enough to buy enough drugs to last them a week.

"Yeah, we can get us a couple ounces and..." Michelle cosigned until the engine came to a grinding halt. "What now?"

"Engine locked up," the mechanic explained an hour later after roadside assistance towed her to the nearest shop.

"Well hurry up and fix it cuz I gotta go into the city," she said doing the crack head antsy dance from foot to foot.

"A seized motor? Hurry up?" he repeated and cracked up. "Ma'am, you're gonna need a whole new motor. That's about six grand and ain't no 'hurry up' to that. It'll be a couple weeks, at best."

"Taxi!" Reese shouted since neither had time for all that. They had the six thousand but that was for cracks, not cars.

"Fuck outta here!" Michelle cosigned with an indignant chuckle. Taxis didn't swim along out here like schools of fish like they did in the city so they had to call one. Then when it came it wasn't cheap like New York city gypsy cabs. "Two hundred dollars! To go to Harlem!"

"Let's use your husband's car? May as well, he dead," Reese suggested. She shrugged her shoulders to make it seem so reasonable that Michelle crossed that line too. Until now she had left his belongings, including his car right where they were.

"Hell yeah," she agreed. The ride home was still fifty bucks but beat two hundred.

Rohan's car started up without hesitation despite sitting for almost a year. Michelle turned the radio up to tune out the memories that came flooding back into her mind. This same vehicle delivered the family to many good times. Now it was the new crack mobile. Both danced with their own devil as they rode into the city and back.

Chapter 9

"Do I have to?" Megan moaned when Wednesday night rolled around a lot quicker than she'd hoped. She also hoped her grandmother would have forgotten about it but Officer Johnson came through last night to remind her. He laid some pipe too, but reminded her of the appointment.

"Yes, you have to!" Dianne insisted. "You need something to do besides looking out the window. You need to get out and do something. Make friends, play, something!"

"Why?" Megan asked cocking her head. She didn't have friends home on Long Island either and was totally fine with her own company.

"Because I said so," she shot back ending the conversation. That statement trumped anything she could come up with so she gave in and stood.

Na-Na was holding court on her bench when Megan stepped from her building. She stopped her chatter to stare her down as she walked through the courtyard. Megan lowered her gaze and didn't look over to the rat pack. They resumed yelling and cursing once she cleared the courtyard. She walked down a few blocks and over one until she made it to the address on the card.

"It stinks in here!" Megan fussed when she walked inside. The funk made her want to turn around but the sounds and sights of violence urged her inside.

The gym was full of people engaged in various work outs and exercises. The ring in the middle caught her eye and drew her near. Inside was a couple vigorously sparing. The light skin man threw vicious combinations that pinned the darker man to the ropes. Body shots that sounded like an African beating a drum and uppercuts that lifted him off his feet. Closer inspection showed one of the men was a woman. An aggressive, hard hitting woman.

"I see you made it," Officer Johnson said coming up behind her ringside. "She's good huh?"

"She's great!" Megan replied through a wide smile as the woman pummeled the man on the ropes. He was literally saved by the bell and the beating came to an abrupt stop.

"What got into you today, O'Neil?" the man asked after he spit out his mouthpiece and pulled off his head gear.

"Got cramps," she said rubbing her glove over her stomach. They bumped gloves as goodbye and separated. She turned and saw Megan and Officer Johnson and came over. "Is this her?"

"This is her. Megan meet Officer Patrica O'Neil. O'Neil, Megan," he said formally introducing the two.

"You're a police officer?" Megan cheered as if she'd met her pop idol. She didn't actually have a pop idol so she was crazy about cops.

"I sure am," she proudly proclaimed. "Johnson tells me you need to learn how to fight?"

"No, I'm fine. Thank you," she declined. She was here because she had to, not to learn how to fight.

"Well she needs to learn how to duck, block or something!" he said with a chuckle and walked off. With Megan here that meant Dianne was almost alone and that meant he was about to get some pussy.

"How old are you, Megan?" Officer O'Neil asked as she led her over to the heavy bags.

"Almost twelve," she said since kids always round up. Her birthday was drawing near but she wasn't looking forward to it. Birthdays and holidays had lost their meaning since she lost her father.

"Well that's a good age. Now, let's see what you got," she said pointing at the large punching bag hanging from a chain. She put a pair of gloves on the girl's hand and stepped back.

"Got what?" she asked in confusion. She looked back and forth from the woman and the bag and asked, "Hit it?"

"Hit it," she said, nodding. "Hit it as hard as you can!"

"Mmph," Megan huffed and threw a girly punch that barely registered.

"What the hell was that?" Officer O'Neil asked twisting her face. "Hit it! Sock it like whoever did that to your eye!"

"Ugh!" she grunted and swung with all her might. The punch sounded off and rocked the heavy bag. It swung away but came back and knocked her down.

"Well damn!" the lady cop chuckled at both the heavy handed punch as well as her getting knocked over. She reached a hand down to help her up, "Now hit it again. This time, stand like this."

"Like this?" Megan asked, mimicking her stance perfectly. The woman pushed her and she kept her balance.

"Just like that!" she nodded. Megan swung another heavy punch that rocked the heavy bag. This time she rolled away when it came back just like Officer O'Neil showed her. The next two hours flew by as she trained the girl. She had a long way to go but was off to a great start.

"Let me get changed and I'll walk you home."

Officer O'Neil didn't wait for a response and hit the locker room. Megan smiled wildly as she realized how much fun she just had. She couldn't wait until Friday so she could come back and train some more. Time flew as she watched the other gym rats doing various exercises. A man on their speed bag caught her eye with his rhythmic beating. It was almost like he was dancing and she wanted to try that next.

"You ready?" a pretty woman with big, bouncy curls framing her face asked as she approached. The woman laughed and shook her head at the confused look on Megan's face. "It's me. Officer O'Neil? Girl, come on!"

"Officer O'Neil?" she asked and squinted. This woman was too girly and curvy to be the same woman who beat dude up in the ring. Nothing was the same except the voice. Megan had to ask again as they walked out getting another laugh out of the officer.

"Girl, come on!" she giggled showing the other side of the coin. Heads was pretty and tails kicked ass. Megan decided just then that she wanted to be her when she grew up.

*****

Michelle still hadn't grown up, shown up, or sent a dime in support of her children. She and Reese partied like rock stars, smoking rocks.

Megan really didn't expect anything for her birthday since things were tight around the house. She got something for her birthday all right, but it wasn't quite what she expected. Or asked for, but an inevitable fact of life.

"Oh man," Megan groaned when she discovered puberty came in her sleep. The smart girl knew what was happening but still called for help.

"Grandmother! Can you come in here? Please," she called as if scared to move.

"Child, what you got going on now? I'm trying to... oh, OK," she said seeing her dilemma. "Go take your shower. I'll wash these sheets."

Megan showered as her grandmother schooled her on the art of womanhood, ghetto style.

"You have to be careful now because you can get pregnant. I got my hands full with your brother already and I ain't trying..."

"He's not my brother," she stuck her head out and reminded. His first birthday was approaching and she still had yet to touch him. She would glare and stare at it but had nothing to do with him.

Megan listened in amusement as her grandmother gave advice on men now that she was a woman. It wasn't quite as amusing as sneaking out and watching her and Officer Johnson having sex but amusing nonetheless.

Megan was still lowering her gaze in school and around the projects to avoid Na-Na. It kept her out of trouble but still didn't sit well with her. Being coward is as unnatural as the two men she saw kissing last night. Luckily for her she didn't see what they did to each other when they went inside the building.

*****

"I got it!" Megan called in response to the knock on the door since she was headed out. It was another Friday night, which meant she was on her way to the gym. It also meant she knew who would be on the other side of the door. "Hello, Officer Johnson."

"Hello, dear. What's so funny?" he asked of her snickers and giggles when she let him inside. She looked him up and down and covered her mouth to laugh some more.

"Nothing," she lied in reply since she couldn't tell him why she was laughing. Seeing him giving her grandmother some late night back shots last night just cracked her up. She grabbed her training bag and giggled her way down the hallway.

"Hey, babes," Dianne announced as she came out from the rear of the apartment. "He's sleep, so come on."

"You ain't gotta tell me twice!" he cheered. His Viagra kicked in on the way over so he was already ready. He dropped his pants allowing his erection to pop free and quiver like a diving board.

"Sit!" she ordered since she had been thinking about riding him all day. She lifted her house dress up and stepped out of her granny panties, then climbed on board. She reached down to wriggle him inside and sink down to the bottom of her box.

"Mm, mm, mph," Johnson said feeling the hot pussy engulf his Johnson. He gripped her hips and held on for the ride.

****

"Can I do the speed bag yet?" Megan practically pleaded as she and Officer O'Neil changed into their gym clothes. The woman didn't shower with the child so this was as much as she would get to see.

Megan would watch, side eye to get a glimpse of her curves. No homo, she just hoped to look like that herself one day. Maybe there was a knockout lurking under the pounds of baby fat she was carrying around. Time would tell since she shed a few pounds with each visit. Not to mention the way Officer O'Neil turned her nose up at cakes and candy caused her to leave it off as well. After all, when you want to be someone you do what they do.

"You're not ready for that yet. We still need to work on defense," Officer O'Neil replied. She was smart enough to know that you can't beat everyone so the next best thing is to prevent anyone from beating you. That meant defense; lots and lots of blocks, ducks and rolling away. Each came with countermoves but she wasn't ready for them yet.

"Yes I am! Test me!" she dared, watching yet another man do his dance on the speed bag. His head nodded along with whatever was coming out his ear buds and his feet stepped in rhythm with the bouncing bag.

"OK, I'm ready. Suit up," Officer O'Neil dared and tossed her some head gear. "If I land one punch, we're starting over."

"From the beginning?" she exclaimed wide eyed in shock. Still the lure of the speed bag held her tightly. "Deal!"

"Deal, huh? She must think I'ma take it easy on her," Officer O'Neil mumbled as they climbed into the ring. Several eyes turned to see who was getting into the ring then turned away seeing it was the chubby girl.

Ding,ding the bell rung and they moved in and tapped gloves. Officer O'Neil snuck a straight jab as soon as they touched gloves. She expected to connect so they could climb right back out of the ring and get back to her routine. Instead Megan dipped under it and rolled away.

"Oh, OK," Officer O'Neil said through her mouthpiece and nodded. Megan kept her guard high and waited. She didn't have to wait long as Officer O'Neil came with a combination of blows. A flurry of lefts, rights, jabs and body shots that got nowhere.

Megan blocked, ducked and dodged the half speed punches just like she'd been taught. Soon they had a crowd as people gathered at ringside to watch. They were treated to quite a show as Megan deflected or ducked everything she threw at her. O'Neil was tempted to go full speed to teach her a lesson but realized she was only carrying out the lessons she already taught.

"OK, now after you duck, side step and shoot an uppercut," she instructed and threw a looping right hand. Megan followed directions and perfected the move. By the end of the session no one her age could whoop her. Not even Na-Na.

Chapter 10

"What now?" Michelle asked once all of her husband's belongings had been smoked. All his jewelry, cameras, tools, weights and etcetera had been sold, cooked then smoked. Not a trace of him ever being here remained. Except his car but that didn't look anything like the well preserved classic it once was.

"Shit... I don't know," Reese replied looking at the TVs, stereos and other valuables that still remained. She had a small stash of items she pilfered and set aside for when this gravy train finally derailed. She was a pro; a crack head's crack head and saw the end quickly approaching. Even she had no idea it was coming as quickly as it did. "Let's sell some of this other stuff. You really need all this furniture?"

"Not really. I really don't need my daughter's furniture," she decided. She could sell the pink pony bedroom for some white cocaine.

"I know that's right. We don't need TVs in her room either," Reese said. She was going to show her how it's done and smoke the whole house.

"Who the fuck is that?" Michelle fussed in reply to her doorbell. She wasn't expecting company so she peeked out the blinds to see who was ringing and knocking at the same time like the police. "Oh shit! Its the police!"

"For what? We ain't did shit!" Reese insisted since they were only stealing from a dead man. She was pretty sure Rohan hadn't reported it. Still she was ready to run out the back door and try her luck in the woods.

"Oh shit! I blew my court date," Michelle suddenly remembered. "Yo, just answer it and tell them I don't stay here. Tell them you haven't seen me and don't know where I am."

"OK girl," Reese said matching her whisper. She waited until Michelle ducked into the closet and closed the door. She smoothed her clothes and pulled the front door open. "Can I help you?"

"We're looking for Michelle Robinson," the cop said holding up a picture to compare it to Reese. He lowered it once he saw at a glance it wasn't her.

"She has a warrant for failure to appear," the other cop announced from behind him. "Is she here? Have you seen her?"

"Yup, I sure have," she said turning and pointing to where she was hiding. "She's in that closet."

The cops paused and looked at each other for a second to see if she was serious or not. Usually people say the fugitive isn't home even if they were. The first one shrugged and stepped in to confirm or deny.

"This bitch," Michelle muttered to herself when she heard her friend sell her out. She heard the footsteps in her direction and braced herself. She knew what she had to do if that door came open. It did and she sprang into action.

"What the fuck!" the startled cop exclaimed as she tore out of the closet in a flash. Luckily the second cop was standing behind him because she had the jump on the first. He would never have caught the nimble crack head had she got by him.

"No you don't!" the second cop announced and tackled her before she could. An adult female crack head can be very strong when cornered and she put up quite a fight. The first cop joined in and helped subdue Michelle. It took some doing but they managed to get her hands behind her back and put the cuffs on her. Both middle aged men were huffing and puffing trying to catch their breath.

"Yo... Why the fuck you sold me out?" Michelle pleaded to Reese once they stood her up. Both cops turned with raised eyebrows waiting to hear the answer themselves.

Reese just shrugged and watched them cart her away. A smile spread on her face as the squad car backed out of the driveway. Now she had the whole house to herself. Michelle would be gone for at least a few months waiting on a court date. That was plenty of time to smoke the rest of the house.

*****

"Look," Yvonne said and pointed at the door of the bodega as Megan came in. The two girls had scrambled up twenty-two cent to share a bag of quarter chips to share.

"Bet she got money," Na-Na said since Megan often did. Officer Johnson always broke Dianne off a few bucks after she broke him off a few nuts. Not prostitution in the classic sense, but more like one hand washing the other. Megan always got a couple dollars out the deal to put in her pocket.

Megan didn't feel like ducking out and walking up the hill to the other store like she usually did when she saw the bully and her sidekick. She didn't feel like lowering her gaze either and lifted her chin instead.

Na-Na saw something was different and really didn't want any parts of it. She could front all she wanted for her friends but she felt the girl's grip and was afraid of her. However peer pressure has been getting kids pregnant, high, drunk and fucked up since the beginning of time. History was about to repeat itself when Yvonne urged her friend on.

"You should take that bitch money! At least make her pay for our chips! We can get a quarter water too!" she whispered like the devil does. " I got yo' back!"

"Yeah," Na-Na said, chomping on the bait. Now she was on the hook and moved toward to confront her.

Megan watched the girls approach from the side as she selected an apple and banana for a snack. She closed her eyes and silently 'wished these bitches would', and they did.

"Hey, fat girl," Na-Na said even though she wasn't nearly as fat as she was when she arrived. "Pay for our shit!"

"No," Megan turned and said with a smile that scared Na-Na. If not for that damn Yvonne she would have said 'OK' and fled.

"Oh hell no! Who this bitch think she talking to? Beat that bitch ass!" the instigator insisted.

It was either Na-Na's low IQ or no will power combined with peer pressure that pressured her to swing on the girl. Megan dipped the punch and stepped aside forcing her to fall into the rack of chips and knock them down.

"Hey, cut the shit!" one of the Puerto Rican clerks demanded from behind the counter. He was about to come out and break it up before they tore his store up.

"Wait, hold up," the other clerk laughed and stopped his brother from stopping the fight. He boxed himself and had to admire the smooth duck. He enjoyed the next one and the ten others that followed as Megan dipped and ducked everything Na-Na threw. "Little Mami got skills!"

"Is that all you got?" Megan asked, growing bored of the lopsided battle. They both knew she could and would hurt the girl if she joined the fight.

"Bitch, you lucky I got my period!" Na-Na shouted. It didn't make much sense but sometimes any excuse will do. This was one of them excuses since she saw she had a 'no win' coming. She said 'fuck them chips' and took off out the store.

"Yo! Where you going?" Yvonne called after Na-Na as she marched out of the store. She frowned at Megan smiling back and followed her friend. "You let that chick punk you out!"

"You got nice moves, Mami," the clerk said nodding when Megan came and paid for her snacks.

"Thank you. I learned at P.A.L," she said proudly. The clerk smiled and nodded again since he learned how to box in that same gym when he was a kid.

****

Megan didn't know what exactly to expect when she returned to the projects. She half expected the gang of girls to jump her but wasn't scared. She would fight them all if she had too because she vowed to never run again. The girls were engaged in an animated argument when she came through the courtyard. This time it was Yvonne in charge. No one wants to be number two and she was ready to be head hood rat in charge.

"There she go now! Do something!" Yvonne dared after telling the pack of rats what happened in the store. Megan looked at Na-Na and this time it was her turn to lower her gaze.

"See! Told you she was pussy!"

"Bitch you pussy!" Na-Na stood and shot back. She had already beat Yvonne up to claim the top spot and would fight her again to keep it. She was going to have to because Yvonne punched her dead in her mouth.

Megan let out a little chuckle as she walked into the building and went upstairs. They could beat each other to death as far as she cared. Neither had any defense so they just leaned their heads back and swung wildly. Whoever could take the most beating wins.

"What them girls fighting about now?" Dianne asked in exasperation when Megan walked in. She heard the commotion in the courtyard and went to the window to be nosey. She was relieved to see Megan wasn't involved this time. "Old Na-Na getting her ass whipped out there!"

"Yeah," she replied since she assumed she would. She was smart enough to know Yvonne would try her next and decided she would be the one. Officer O'Neil told her she wouldn't have to beat the whole crew up, just one. Just beat the shit out of one of them and they wouldn't ever bother her again. The phone rang preventing her from joining her grandmother in the window. She picked it up and took the call, "Hello?"

'You have a collect call from an inmate in the Nassau County jail. Caller, state your name, 'Michelle'. To accept press...

"Who was that?" Dianne frowned matching Megan's frown when she hung up the phone. She was expecting a call from Officer Johnson to set up a date to ride on his Johnson.

"Nobody," Megan spat in an attitude she borrowed from a girl in her third period class. The ghetto child would roll her eyes, bat her eyes and lift her head to the side when she didn't like something. Megan imitated it better than she did it herself.

"I got it!" her grandmother huffed when the phone rang again. Megan sat down and waited to get scolded for hanging up on her mother. Her brother stared curiously at her like he always did. The toddler gave up on trying to get attention from her. Now he just stared. Megan stuck her tongue out at him and turned back to Dianne.

"I know you didn't just hang up on me!" Michelle barked when her mother accepted the expensive collect call.

"I... " Dianne tried to reply but her abusive, abrasive daughter went in before she had a chance to explain.

"Look, that bitch Reese got me lock up," she began. It was only partially true since she was the one who blew off her court date. Reese just sold her out when the cops came knocking. "I'm going before the judge in the morning."

"Same judge as last time?" she interrupted at the risk of getting cursed out. She remembered the stern warning she received last time.

"Yeah. Tell them I got a new born and I breastfeed and..." she rambled. Her mother couldn't help but to cut in once more.

"Jax is almost a year old. He can walk and everything," Dianne informed her. The silence that followed was because Michelle strained to recall how long she'd been gone. Time flies when having fun, but really, really flies when smoking crack all day.

"He is?" she asked incredulously. Another silence followed as she searched her raggedy mind for a solution. "How 'bout that cop you was fucking? See if he can pull some strings and get me out this bitch."

"OK, baby. Mmhm, OK," she repeated watching the clock, hoping the fifteen minutes would hurry by. It took fifteen minuets of crack head ramblings before time expired. "OK, baby. I'll see you soon. Bye."

"What she want? We gotta go to court?" Megan asked twisting her lips to show what she thought of the idea. Little Jax turned his face to and fro to face whoever was speaking.

"No. Your mother needs some rest and she's about to get some," Dianne said with a sigh. She knew the suburbs of Long Island were stricter than the five boroughs of New York City. Those drug charges were going to cost Michelle a couple of years upstate. The three months sitting in county didn't help so maybe a few years would.

Chapter 11

"So, how's school?" Officer O'Neil asked as Megan beat on the speed bag. She mastered it once she finally got her chance to get to it. Hers was a combination of what she saw, and learned with a little of her own flavor.

"Good. I, found, the, one," she informed in rhythm with her beating. When she left the projects Yvonne was sitting on the top of the bench, otherwise known as the throne, while the other girls sat below on the seat or stood around. Na-Na was sporting two black eyes standing off to the side.

"Well always try for a peaceful solution. Violence should be a last resort," she advised. Megan didn't reply so she stepped in and stopped the bag to repeat herself. "I said..."

"I heard you but that girl doesn't want peace. She wants a piece and I'm going to give it to her," Megan vowed. The days of being bullied were over.

Yvonne was a bigger bully than Na-Na had been. Where Na-Na would glare, Yvonne would yell curses and threats. She vowed to take her money next time she saw her at the store. Megan secretly wished she would try her and was about to get her wish.

"How's your mom?" the cop asked to switch the subject as they switched over to the heavy bags. Megan threw some heavy punches that proved this was just as touchy a subject. She rocked the large bag with heavy haymakers as Officer O'Neil held on.

"I, don't know. She, keeps, calling but, we, don't take, her calls," she replied still in rhythm while rocking the large bag. She was denied bond as the judge promised but had another court date soon.

"Good work, mama. Lets get dressed and I'll walk you home," Officer O'Neil said bringing the session to a close.

Fifteen minutes later they headed out of the gym for the walk over to the projects. They stopped by the bodega for snacks of apples and bananas. Megan turned her nose up defiantly as they passed the cakes and chips she once loved.

"Anything else, pretty lady?" the smooth clerk asked Officer O'Neil flirtatiously.

"No, thank you," she giggled and cooed coyly. Megan twisted her face and looked up at her curiously. As soon as they left the store she reverted back to her usual self.

"You like that guy?" she had to ask. She couldn't help but notice the change in demeanor when she dealt with him; the smile, batting of eyes and flip of her hair. All moves Megan would practice later in front of the mirror.

"He's cute but we're in different worlds. Can't get caught up in a man I may have to put the cuffs on one day," she replied. The perplexed look on the girl's face told her she said too much. Luckily there was a distraction ahead to change to subject for her.

"That's the one," Megan said pointing at Yvonne. It was bait and the girl quickly took it and stood.

"I know she ain't talking about me? Yo, you got something to say, say it to my face!" she fussed and came near. "Yo' moms can't save you either!"

"Moms! I look old enough to be her mother?" Officer O'Neil reeled vainly. She wanted to pull her mirror from her purse to check but this obviously wasn't the time. "Yeah, she the one."

"Told you," Megan said as they squared up. "We may as well get this over wi..."

"Ugh!" Yvonne interrupted her speech with a sucker punch. Megan had seen her sneak enough girls to know it was coming. She ducked under the punch and unleashed a three shot body blow combination that made Yvonne's period come on two days early.

Technically the fight was over at that point. Yvonne lost her will to fight once she felt her power. It left along with all the breath from her body from the body shots. However, she was the one and she was going to take a beating. Megan lumped her up with jabs to stall until a big enough crowd gathered. Once the courtyard was sold out she popped the top on the can of 'whoop ass' she had.

Collective 'oohs', 'aahs' and 'oh shits' played background to the thuds of the heavy blows. Plenty of men, women, boys and girls had gotten beat up in this spot but none as bad as this. Yvonne saw an uppercut speeding towards her and welcomed it. She knew it would end the fight and it did.

"OK, that's enough!" Officer O'Neil fussed and stopped Megan from stomping the unconscious girl. She frowned at the faraway look in the girl's eyes. It was a blank look that gave the cop a shiver up her spine. "Let's go upstairs."

*****

A few more months had sped by and it was time for Michelle to go before the judge once again. Dianne had blocked her abusive calls but still made it a point to come to her court date. She brought little Jax along with a defiant Megan.

"I don't know why I have to miss school for her," she spat as they rode the train as far as it would take them. Next would be a long bus ride out to the Nassau County courthouse.

"How 'bout cuz I said so!" Dianne snapped. She loved that her granddaughter had came out of her sheltered shell even if it meant having to check her from time to time. It really bothered her that the girl still wouldn't have anything to do with her brother. She did finally stop calling him 'it', now he was just 'him'.

Michelle's public defender assured her that if she pled guilty to the possession charges she would get probation, possibly treatment classes but no jail time. It was true in the case of the middle aged white women caught with prescription pills, but not black people with crack.

Michelle spotted her family when she came from the holding cell and entered the courtroom. Guilt made her angry so she turned her face away and lifted her chin defiantly. Little Jax didn't register her presence since he didn't know who she was. He was only a few hours old when he last saw her.

"Pfft, I'm missing school for this?" Megan grumbled. Dianne gave her a side eye but remained quiet. She recognized the defiance for what it really was, pain; the pain of being abandoned by your own mother. She knew it well from having done it to her own daughter. She took the weight of the blame for Michelle sitting at the defendant table.

"Robinson, Michelle. Case number..." the clerk said announcing her case. There was a brief silence as the judge looked down and reviewed his notes on the case.

"Uh oh," the public defender said when the judge raised his brows. He then raised his head and glared down at the women who said the drugs belonged to her ten year old daughter.

"How does the defendant plead?" he dared, cocking his head back and to the side. He had ten years he could give on the drugs and five for the other charges. He would run them wild for a total of fifteen if she said anything other than...

"Guilty, your honor," the public defender blurted out quickly. She heard her client was quite impulsive and combative. Michelle had smoked all reason away and was on the cusp of mental illness.

"Oh, OK," the judge nodding like 'bitch better plead guilty'. "I hereby sentence her to fifteen years, with five to serve. The reminder of the sentence will be suspended in lieu of intense probation."

"So I can go?" Michelle asked her public defender after the judge banged his gavel. People tend to only hear what they want to hear and all she heard was the word 'probation'.

"Un huh. Sure you can," the woman replied. She left out the part about five years but she was going home eventually.

"Wow," Megan heard herself exclaim when she processed the sentence. This was the same amount of time Jax got for killing her father.

"It's for the best. Your mom needs help," Dianne said gently. She too had to process it and realized the baby would be in first grade when she came home and Megan would almost be grown.

Megan didn't care but didn't say so. She got up behind her grandmother and followed her out of the courtroom.

"Hey, baby," Officer Johnson greeted when the family stepped outside of the courthouse. "I took half a day so I could come."

"You always come for me," Dianne giggled, assuming she was speaking over the girl's head. She realized she wasn't when Megan shook her head with a grimace on her face.

"Can we go to my house and get some of my stuff?" she asked since she kept promising she would get Officer Johnson to drive them one day. They were already on the Island which cut the drive in half. Dianne looked at Officer Johnson since it was his decision.

"Sure. What's the address?" he asked. She answered and they set off towards Suffolk County.

Megan felt a wave of melancholy when the sights became so familiar. It increased when they reached her subdivision and peaked when they reached her block. Then crashed and burned when they reached the house.

"Is this it?" Officer Johnson scrunched his face and asked.

"I don't think so?" Dianne asked looking for the numbers on the fancy mailbox. She didn't see the ornate box and shook her head 'no'. "This isn't it."

"Yes it is," Megan said sadly and got out. She looked at the shell of what use to be her happy home, her happy life and broke. Not externally in tears and sobs. No, something snapped internally and that's far worse.

The house was far worse as well. The shutters and siding were gone from the walls. The fancy front door was also missing so she didn't need her key. The expensive carpet was pulled up and the appliances were pulled out. So was the furnace, air conditioner and cabinets. Granite counters gone, wrought iron stair rails gone. The walls were all busted so the copper pipes could be gutted as well.

"What happened here?" Officer Johnson asked as he came in behind her. Megan unfroze and walked down the hall to her bedroom. She just shook her head at what once was because it was all gone.

"Reese did this!" Dianne declared. She picked the house down to the bone like a piece of chicken. "You should lock her ass up!"

"I would if I could," Johnson replied truthfully. The truth of the matter was this wasn't his jurisdiction plus they had no proof. The only thing he could do was hit the home improvement store to board up their missing windows and doors.

*****

Megan sat up in the window but didn't pay much attention to the happenings down below. The usual suspects were doing the usual suspicious shit on a Saturday night in the projects. It was so monotonous it was almost predicable. She saw something scurry by that was bigger than the large Norway rats that lived amongst them. It caught her attention so she zoomed in and focused.

"Reese," Megan growled when she recognized her. It took some doing since she didn't look much like her old self. Her voluptuous body had went up in smoke leaving nothing but a big head junky on a frail junky body behind. She'd lost her apartment during her stay out on Long Island and now had nowhere to go. She would float around these projects like a ghost until she was a real ghost.

"Get yo' ass away from here," Lil Wop fussed and gave her a kick in her ass to get her started. She tricked with all the dealers once today so they now wanted cash.

"Yo, come here," a man called as he walked through the courtyard. He just got off night shift and decided a quick blowjob would help him sleep. Good decision since a good blowjob is the best sleep aid known to man.

"Twenty bucks?" she asked hopefully as she hopped over to him.

"Yeah right!" he said getting a good laugh out of it. "I got five on it."

"Sold!" she said accepting the job. It would get her a nick to smoke and that's better than nothing. They stepped inside the staircase of Megan's building and she couldn't help not to go investigate.

Megan used her junior cop skills to ease out of her room. She listened to her grandmother's soft snores and slid down the hall. It took some doing to unlock their locks without making noise but she got it done and slipped out of the apartment.

'Sslp, ugh, ugh', Megan heard when she eased into the staircase. The sound of the blowjob carried up the cinder blocks wall like the urine and weed smoke. She crept down and watched Reese gagging as the man happily humped her face.

"Shit, shit, shit!" he cursed and went stiff. He grabbed Reese's big head and held her in place while he skeeted down her throat. He rotated his hips and grinded as if in some pussy as he got off. "Mmm."

"I should get a tip," she proclaimed after swallowing a week worth of pent up frustration.

"You just got one!" he chuckled as he put his dick away. He produced the agreed upon fiver and departed. He went home and she was home since she was homeless. Megan couldn't resist the temptation and rushed down the steps.

"What the... oh, hey girl. You Michelle's daughter, ain't you? Let me hold five dollars," she said when confronted. Megan didn't come to give her money. Instead she rattled off a five punch combination that dropped the crack head on her ass. A kick removed a couple of loose teeth that really needed to come out anyway.

Megan would have kept beating her had she stuck around. She didn't though and scrambled to her feet and took off.

"These mine," Megan said collecting the teeth with an empty potato chip bag. She tossed them down the trash shoot when she reached her floor and eased back inside. That was the best sleep she had since leaving home.

Chapter 12

Time flies whether you're having fun or not. It seems life was on autopilot once I settled into my new life in New York City. It seems like just yesterday that my dad was tucking me in and reading bedtime stories.

"You are so pretty!" Dianne exclaimed when her now sixteen-year-old granddaughter emerged for breakfast. It wasn't an empty compliment since the once chubby girl had blossomed into a beautiful young woman.

She inherited east Indian hair from her father that she kept pulled into a curly pony tail. It had thick waves cascading back like a calm lake disturbed by a rock. Increasing her workouts from two to four days a week had chiseled all the baby fat away leaving a stunning shapely shape that turned heads everywhere she went. The only thing fat on her now was her round ass that jetted out from flat stomach and waist.

"Thank you, grandma. I get it from you," she replied spreading a smile on the woman's face.

"You are pretty," Jax said between bites of his breakfast cereal.

"So are you," she shot back and snarled. The cute boy had his father's charm and finally won his half sister over. "Pretty lame that is!"

"You too are something else," Dianne fussed as they bantered back and forth. She was just relieved the girl's cold heart softened towards the boy. It had taken five years but she finally came around. Still wouldn't call him by his name though. She would make up new names for him daily but never Jax.

"Well come on, Randy. Let's go" Megan said grabbing some fruit for breakfast. She was in the habit of walking Jax to school before catching the bus to the train for the ride to school.

Jax Junior and Dianne shook their heads and said their good bye for the day. They exited the apartment and headed towards the staircase. Both instinctively took deep breaths and held them for the sprint down the steps and outside. Reese almost jumped out of her skin when she saw the girl and took off.

"Why does she always do that?" her little brother asked scrunching his face.

"Don't do your face like that!" she fussed since he looked just like his father when he did.

"Thank you. I don't know. She a crack head."

"Oh," he replied even though he didn't quite understand what the term meant. Whatever it was the projects were full of them.

"Sup, Megan," Yvonne called out as she strolled through the courtyard pushing her son in a stroller. Her daughter was due in a few weeks giving her a waddle in her walk.

"Sup, yo," she replied in her ghetto girl persona. She'd watched each and everyone of the girls from the bench have at least one kid. They all smoked menthols and weed now that they were grown. The older teen boys watched them blossom and bloom into young women and rushed to stick their dicks in them.

Na-Na had a child by Grip and was pregnant by Lil Wop who had a baby by Yvonne. It was a love octagon stemming from bench to bench and consummated in staircases and rooftops.

By now Megan had amassed quite a collection of characters. She did a spot on Jamaican girl as well as valley girl. She could be white, black, Latino or Asian. Hood, suburban, professional, young or old. She mastered Spanish and ebonics switching up with whoever she came across.

"A'ight, Maurice. Have a good day. Be safe and learn," Megan said stopping short of giving her brother a hug or kiss.

"Mr. Jackson," Jax said as he departed. Even he knew she would never call him by name but never would know why.

*****

Megan ended up going to a vocational high school in Manhattan. Her great grades and theatrics got her noticed by teachers who recommended her for the school. They thought she'd be a star one day but all she wanted was a badge and gun.

She wasn't particularly into boys since they didn't fit in her immediate plans but boys sure were interested in. Men too and a few women once she blossomed. She wasn't even in full bloom yet but her ass and tits pushed her clothes out in all the right directions.

"Dang, ma! What's good, love? Let me get your math!" a young goon exclaimed when her saw her display in the tight jeans. He came around front and made his request for her phone number.

"No hablo English," she replied and turned away. Turned away right into the smiling face of a Puerto Rican.

"Dame tu numbre," he said speaking her language. She switched to Arabic with a clever laugh but a young Arab man was right there as well.

"Kayfa halik? Ma' asmuk?" he asked shooting his shot at the pretty girl.

"Ugh!" Megan grunted and stormed off. This was a typical ride to school in New York City. She usually buried her face in a book to distract attention and be distracted. As soon as she sat and opened her book a girl called her name.

"Megan? Is that you?" a gorgeous East Indian girl asked and cocked her head to help make the identification. It obviously worked because she decided it was. "It is you!"

"Um..." Megan wondered if she was having a gay moment because the girl was beautiful. Beautiful and familiar. She twisted her lips and put a hand on a shapely hip. Her tight pants gave a perfect impression of the plump camel toe underneath.

"It's Angel! Your cousin!" she squealed and bounced causing her breast to bounce along with her. Megan didn't have to squint or cock her head since she looked just like her dead mom looked in life.

"Oh my God! Angel!" she squealed, hopped up the hug her long lost cousin. "How's grandma?"

"Mean and nasty as ever! She be cock blocking and shit," she replied.

The nosey train riders watched the girls laugh and get reacquainted. They ended their reunion when Angel's stop approached. The girls exchanged numbers and promised to hang out first chance they got. That chance came a couple of weeks later when a long awaited movie finally dropped.

*****

"And just where are you going looking all, all... grown?" Dianne asked when Megan emerged from her room. Most Friday nights she would leave in sweats for the gym but today she had on her good jeans and good shirt. Not having much money meant not having much clothes. Dianne did splurge on her grandchildren to have a few nice outfits for special occasions. This was obviously one of them since she was dressed up as high as her limited wardrobe would allow.

"Me and Angel are going to 161st to catch a movie," she replied. Jax eyes went wide at the sound of movies since they didn't get to go much.

"Ooh, can I go?" he popped up from his trucks and action figures and pleaded back and forth between the two.

"Sorry, Charlie," Megan giggled. She was quite pleased that she'd yet to call him by his right name or the same wrong name twice.

"How you get money for movies?" her grandmother dared with a frown. She clearly remembered when her daughter began dressing nice and hanging out. Michelle was fucking far and wide by this age once she discovered the value of vagina. Hers was like a credit card redeemable for cash, weed, coke, movies or whatever.

"I didn't buy lunch today and Angel is paying," she explained. Megan understood why the woman was so strict on her. She had a pile of unopened letters from her mother as proof of what being too lenient can produce. Had she opened and read any of them she would have seen how sorry and repentant her mother was. She vowed to do better and be better when she came home.

"OK, have fun. Me and your brother gonna have to play some poker," Dianne shrugged.

"Oh Lord! Watch your allowance Smitty!" she laughed and sashayed her pretty ass out of the apartment and down the hall. Right down the pissy stairs and out into the courtyard. Her jeans were too tight not to pass by the dope boys. She may not have fed into the cat calls and 'come ons', but she didn't mind the attention.

"Damn, ma! That ass is fat!" Grip said standing to give the round cheeks a round of applause. That set off a standing ovation that cracked the cute girl up.

"Y'all be bugging!" she laughed in her ghetto girl persona. She put a little extra sway in her hips for them on her way over to the girls on their bench. It was the least she could do since they would never, ever get to touch her. "Sup, yo. What y'all doing tonight?"

"We just chilling," Yvonne replied while Na-Na and the others nodded so it would be true. This was where they were born, their children born and probably where they would die. Chilling.

"Oh, OK. Me and my cousin about to catch a flick. I'll holla when I get back," Megan said, nodding even though it wasn't true. These girls were as far as they were going in life and she didn't want to get drug down with them.

Megan was too frugal to spend money catching a bus or cab down the hill to 161st street so she set off on foot. Years of training in the gym not only gave her a great shape, she was also in great shape. She used the gravity of the hill to reach the bottom in no time. A few blocks later she spotted Angel standing in front of the pizza shop they were supposed to meet.

"Look at you, mama!" Angel cheered seeing her cute cousin looking cute.

"Me? Look at you!" she replied seeing Angel's short skirt that barely covered her crotch. She had no shame in her game so Megan blushed for her. "You ready to go in?"

"The question is are you ready to go in?" Angel shot back and waved her hand. Megan turned to see who she was talking to as a souped up SUV pulled up to the curb.

"Who's that?" Megan asked since it was obvious she knew the older guys. They were only in their early twenties but that was plenty old for Megan.

"That's Rico behind the wheel," she said gushing over the pretty thug smiling at her. She went on to explain the pretty passenger as, "Walt, he's yours."

"Mine?" she reeled as Angel rustled her into the back seat.

"Sup, ma? I'm Walt," he exclaimed as Angel and Rico tongue kissed audibly. They smacked and chewed as their tongues wrestled in each others mouth.

"I thought we were going to the movies?" Megan asked, pulling her cousin back to her.

"We are, mama. Not this whack theatre tho'. We going to 42nd street," Walt announced. Megan wanted to protest but Rico already pulled from the curb into traffic.

Megan scrambled to process her thoughts along with her reality. She told her grandmother she was going to the movies so, technically it wasn't a lie. She shook her head when they crossed the 159th bridge into Manhattan since she hadn't told her that.

"Spark up!" Rico ordered, passing a beat up looking blunt to Angel. Megan opened her mouth to make the proclamation that they didn't smoke but her cousin quickly put a flame to the end of it and inhaled.

"Oh, one for you too, cutie," Walt said passing one to Megan as well. Actually passing it at her since she adamantly declined and leaned away.

"No, thank you!" she said with all the force of a child of a crack head. She made a vow to never use drugs, alcohol or tobacco after seeing her mother destroyed by them.

"More for me," he shrugged and lit it himself. He turned the music up as they rode downtown to iconic forty second street.

"Don't, be, so square. They, some, ballers!" Angel managed to warn through tokes of weed. The small time dealers had a pocket full of cash and a used SUV with high miles and chrome rims. Ballers to young, broke chicks like Angel, but it didn't really impress Megan.

The spirals of waves in Walt's hair did though. So did his smile and his smell and she'd never admit it but she even dug his...

"Yo, ma. What y'all trying to see?" he turned and asked in that voice that sent a shiver through her being.

"Huh?" Megan asked. She was too caught up in watching his lips move to catch the question. He chuckled making her vagina throb for the first time in her young life, and repeated the question.

"Shit, don't matter to me!" Angel replied and danced in her seat. She was good and high already and didn't plan on watching it anyway since she came to make out.

"How about Chronicles of a Killa?" Rico cheered. He came to make out as well but the previews had him open.

"Oh hell yeah! Hell yeah!" Walt cheered like a Killa groupie.

"That's what's up!" Megan agreed since she was with Walt. Rico found parking under twenty bucks an hour and pulled in. Once they found a spot they walked towards the theatre district.

"Yo, lets pop in here," Rico suggested as he led the way. It was obvious he was the leader when Walt followed instantly.

"Oh hells yeah!" Angel cheered so happily Megan had to look up at the sign to see what its was.

"Oh hells no!" Megan balked at entering the sex shop. An amazing array of dildos filled the front window and she'd seen enough. She would have seen even more had she went inside.

"I'll wait out here with my cuz," Angel said pulling from under his arm and stepping aside. Rico shrugged and led his follower inside. "Why you bugging, yo?"

"Bugging how? Thems your people, yo. I'on even know them niggers!" she shot back in her ghetto girl routine.

"Girl, I'm telling you they got bread. You better get in where you fit in!" she warned. Megan turned to take in the sights of the tourist spot until the guys returned.

"A'ight, yo! Let's get on this Killa shit!" Rico announced when they returned with bags in hand.

"Ooh, what you got?" Angel squealed and snatched his bag. She giggled girlishly and blushed when she saw the contents. He had all kind of gels, creams and accessories to get his dick sucked but not a single rubber.

The double daters had no choice but to sit next to each other in the packed theatre since the world had been waiting years for Killa to grace the big screen.

"No homo," Rico said when his partner tried to sit beside him with Angel on the other.

"Oh yeah," he said indicating trouble in his future. As a dope boy a prison bid was somewhere in his future and if he had to be told 'no homo' it would probably be homo one day.

Megan sat between the two men with Angel beside Rico. She leaned over, smiled and waved for a split second before he stuck his tongue back down her throat. Megan grimaced at the public display of affection. As soon as the lights went out public went pubic.

"Sup, ma? Let a nigga get a kiss or something," Walt whispered and leaned in. No chick said no yet so he leaned in for one with his lips puckered.

"Um, nope," Megan laughed and blocked his pretty lips from touching her. She wouldn't mind kissing him but not this soon. "Watch the movie, yo."

Megan tried to watch the movie herself but the hot and heavy petting session next to her stole her attention. Her eyes adjusted to the darkness in time to see Rico's hand slip under her short skirt.

"Sss," Angel hissed when his fingers reached her sopping wet vagina. She parted her legs a little so he could get the digits inside of her. The pleasure was too much for her to focus on kissing so she leaned her head back and closed her eyes. "Mmm, you gonna, sss, make me cum."

"Cum then," he demanded in a whisper and worked his fingers a little quicker to send her over the edge. She clamped her mouth on his shoulder and bust a whimpering, shivering nut all over his hand.

"Shit, that could be us," Walt reminded and tried for another kiss. This one got the same results as the first.

"Chill," she said ducking the kiss and knocking his arm away. Killa was doing that Killa shit on the screen but Megan was more interested in the show next to her. Especially when the dick came out.

"Mm-mm," Angel giggled and declined when he tried to guide her head down. Instead she wrapped her dainty hand around his dick and pulled it up and down with a twist of her wrist.

"Kiss it," he pleaded urgently. So urgently Megan was on his side and hoped she would. She sure liked watching sex to be such a prude. As long as it wasn't her pussy she didn't mind. Someone needed to say 'no homo' to Walt again because he was watching the show too.

"Mm-mm," she declined once more. She compromised by spitting on his dick and using it as lube. "I'll do it when we get uptown."

"That's what's up," he agreed. Soon his legs began to rock and his breathing grew choppy. Megan knew he was either about to die or cum, but bet on cuming. "'Bout to buss, ma!"

Megan grimaced when thick globs of cum erupted from his dick. The first one landed on the fitted cap worn by the dude in front of him. The next shot hit the seat and the rest landed on her hand and his jeans.

"Yo, Megan," Walt said pulling Megan's hand. She was too focused on Rico's wood she didn't know what was going on until she felt some meat in her own hand.

"What the... nigga!" she snapped and punched him in his ear so hard he heard bells ringing off in the distance. The blow was so hard he was confused where it came from until Rico helped out.

"Yooo! That bitch punched the shit out of you!" he laughed. The laughter stung just as much as the punch. The laughter that awaited him when they got back to the block is what stirred him to stand to redeem himself. He probably should have stayed seated though. Megan hopped up too, ready to fight.

"You bugging, Megan! Sit down!" Angel shouted. She'd waited months for her turn with the projects dope boy and her cousin was about to fuck it up.

Walt didn't really want to fight a girl, too, but his friend was still laughing at him. He threw a weak jab designed to sit her ass down so they could catch the rest of the movie. Megan ducked and let a body blow fly. It doubled him over to where a nasty knee was heading.

"Oh shit! Yoooo!" Rico laughed louder when his friend fell back in his chair. He contemplated getting back up but knew that meant getting his ass kicked some more. The decision between a good ass kicking and a good movie is always an easy one.

"You bugging," he declared with the air that didn't get knocked out his body and turned to watch the movie. Megan turned to her cousin, ready to leave.

"Come on, Angel. We out!" she demanded making her way out of the asles. Everyone seen her beat dude up leaned back and moved their legs so she could pass.

"Out where? Chill Megan!" she pleaded. "You bugging, yo! Just chill!"

"You... I... well stay here with them then!" she huffed and stormed off.

"You going with her?" Rico dared, knowing she wasn't. He knew she'd been sweating him for a while before he made it around to her. As soon as he got his weight up he went on a vagina tour of their projects.

"Nooo, I wanna stay with you. Remember I'm 'sposed to do that for you!" she said, sealing the deal with some head.

"A'ight, but you gotta let my man hit, too. You the one who brought that crazy bitch..." he reminded. Walt turned his head to catch her reply.

"OK," she agreed somberly. She wanted him so bad she accepted his friend. Pretty much the same way her mother had her first train ran on her at 17. There would be many more in her future, just like her mother.

Chapter 13

"I'm bugging? I'm bugging! No, you bugging!" Megan repeated to herself as she rode the subway train back up to the Bronx. A bum sitting across from her scratched his matted hair as if he didn't talk to himself all day, every day. "You got a problem, yo?"

"No," he said raising his hands in surrender and changing seats away from her. She repeated the statement over and over until she reached her stop. She was livid that her family chose some guy over her. Even she knew the dude would dump her as soon as he got what he wanted. She'd seen and heard it enough times from her window to know exactly how it played out.

Megan squinted as she processed the lessons she learned from the night. She ascertained that men want to come by any means. That's the goal, the finish line. Rico wanted some head but settled for some hand. He would have gladly fucked her underarm pit if he could get a nut. She tucked that tidbit of info away with all the other life lessons she'd gleaned during her short life. She emerged from the underground train onto 161st street and looked around.

"Taxi?" a creepy looking man asked from his creepy looking sedan. Dianne used the bootleg taxis known as gypsy cabs all the time but he gave her the creeps.

"No, I'm not in the mood to be raped and murdered tonight, but thanks," she quipped and started off up the hill. She usually used the incline to train by running up the hill but decided to walk to gather her thoughts. Good thing she did because grandma needed the few extra minutes.

"Get it, get it!" Dianne urged over her shoulder to Officer Johnson and arched her back so he could get it. "Mmm, go on and get it."

"I got it!" he assured her. His bad knee was cooperative tonight allowing him to indulge in some good back shots. He got it too causing the old lady to come all over his old dick. That was his cue to release that nut he'd been holding back for several minutes. A gentleman always waits for a lady to come first or at least together.

"Mmm, baby," Dianne purred like a satisfied kitten. She gave him a kegel squeeze before falling away. A lady always grabs a soapy wash cloth to wash balls so she headed for the door.

"I know, right," he laughed and got off the bed. He accepted the wash cloth when she returned from the bathroom and washed his equipment.

"Aww," she whined in mourning when he pulled his draws on. It was always sad to see him go but understood he had a wife at home. Half a man was better than no man in her book so she didn't complain.

"Don't worry. I'll come through tomorrow," he assured her and kissed her forehead. "Hope my knee don't start acting up."

"Me too!" she cheered and leaned up to kiss his lips. The lip lock almost led to round three until he pulled away. Dianne walked him to the door and got another kiss. She let out a love sick sigh as she watched him walk down the hallway. She finally closed the door when he disappeared into the stairwell.

"Hey, Megan!" he greeted cheerfully when he came across the girl coming up the stairs.

"Hello, Officer Johnson," she sang and giggled. They bumped fist as they passed but the cop stayed put. He listened for the apartment door to open, then close before moving on.

"You home?" Dianne asked rhetorically when Megan entered. A smile stifled the smart Alec remark on the tip of her tongue. The grandmother shook her head knowing she was a smart ass. "Have fun?"

"Not as much as you did." she giggled again and went to the room she now shared with her brother. Force of habit led her to the window to see if she could see anything. She saw Officer Johnson approach the dealers on the bench.

"You boys just gonna do that right in my face, huh?" he asked as Grip made a sale right in his face while smoking a blunt.

"We live here, nigga. You just passing through," he said with an arrogant snarl.

"I... boy. Don't make me lock your ass up!" he warned. He really didn't care about them slinging dope to dope fiends. All he wanted was a little respect.

"Bruh, you don't run shit around here. Now beat it before you get your old ass knocked out," he warned and stood.

"Uh oh," Megan laughed to herself as she watched the situation go from bad to worse. She knew the old man had a mean fight game from watching him in the gym. They couldn't beat him if they all jumped him, so he was in trouble trying to fight him one on one.

Grip threw a couple of looping punches the man easily slipped. Officer Johnson laughed at his feeble punches and popped him in his mouth with a short jab.

"OK, now go on home," Officer Johnson warned after busting his bottom lip. Grip was humiliated and threw a flurry of wild punches. The trained cop ducked and blocked them until he let an old school, left-right combination fly and dropped him on his ass. "Now stay down!"

Grip knew he had no wins with the hands and stayed down. The cop fussed them out for a second but arrested no one. As soon as he turned to leave Grip stood and pulled a pistol from the bushes. They usually kept their drugs and guns there so they couldn't be charged with them since they weren't on their body.

Watch out Megan thought to herself as things went into slow motion. She watched as he rushed up behind the cop and raised the gun. Officer Johnson heard footsteps and spun just in time to see the flash of light that turned out his lights forever. "Nooo!"

"What! I didn't pee!" little Jax exclaimed when her screams snatched him from his sleep. He was at that age and peed the bed often. A check confirmed he did it again. "Shit!"

"Go back to sleep!" she demanded and rushed from the room. She burst into Dianne's room screaming, "Grandma! Wake up! Grandma!"

"Girl what?" she fussed from being pulled from a dick induced coma. "What's wrong!"

"Officer Johnson! He... got shot!" she shouted. Her eyes went wide when her grandmother rolled over and grabbed a pistol from her nightstand. She grabbed her robe and rushed out of the apartment.

Enough people were up to see the shooting to call the police. The report of an officer down had half the precinct enroute.

"Oh no, baby. Get up, baby" Dianne moaned. The pool of blood flowing from the hole in his head told her he would not be getting back up now or ever.

Megan glanced around the crowd of gathering spectators. Grip and his cronies were among them to ensure no one would snitch. It worked too because soon detectives scoured the crowd but no one saw nothing.

"What happened?" Officer O'Neil demanded when she arrived on the scene an hour later. She hopped off her boyfriend's dick when she got the call and rushed over with a fresh batch of semen swimming in her.

"I... I, um, I didn't see anything," she decided but didn't know why. Officer Johnson was family and she couldn't explain why she wouldn't cooperate. It wasn't the code of the streets since she wasn't of the streets and didn't subscribe to its laws.

She had a biblical law in mind. An eye for an eye, life for a life.

****

"Ugh! Ugh! Umph!" Megan get grunted as she pounded the heavy bag with tears streaming down her pretty face. It sounded off so loud several of the gym rats turned to watch.

"That's right, pound it out!" Officer O'Neil urged as she held the bag. Officer Johnson was like a father to her as well but she knew how close he was to the girl and grandmother. Polygyny isn't legal on the books but many men have more than one wife and family to take care of. It's not about the sex most times, but taking care of orphans and widows.

"Did y'all get any tips yet?" she asked contemplating calling the tip line herself. She could certainly use the crime stoppers reward but knew her family would be endangered if she were labeled a snitch. She'd seen many get stitches, cast and body bags for snitching.

"No, but he used a rare gun. A 32 caliber magnum. Not a lot of those floating around," O'Neil relayed. It was police only information but Megan was practically a cop already.

"Speaking of guns, you wanna come to the range with me?"

"When?" Megan asked nodding and bouncing. Officer Johnson had been promising to take her one day but that day wasn't coming.

"I'm going when I leave here," she replied and decided to cut the training short for the evening. "Come on, let's bounce."

Megan usually waiting until she got home to shower but since she wasn't going home she decided to shower in the locker room. She was far too prissy to go anywhere sweaty.

She tried not to watch as Officer O'Neil stripped out of her sweats but she was talking so she paid attention to what she was saying. As best she could anyway, since her eyes darted up and down her curvy frame. It amazed Megan how feminine she was under the masculine grey sweat pants and shirt. A pair of caramel ass cheeks hung from the bottom of her French cut panties. An equally impressive pair of plump breast protruded from the matching bra. Megan instantly decided she wanted her bras and panties to match too from now on.

"So, I made detective. I know Johnson had something to do with it," Officer O'Neil said as she stepped out of her panties. Megan stole a glance between her legs and decided she wanted a bald vagina too. It was a clinical curiosity as opposed to sexual. She needed lessons on being a woman and Dianne was her only role model. As much as she adored the woman she knew she produced Michelle and didn't want to turn out like her.

Megan missed three quarters of what she was saying because she was too busy studying her. She washed her face, body and box in the same order as Officer O'Neil did. She dried and applied lotion just like she did and got dressed.

"I wanna be a detective, too!" Megan announced when Officer O'Neil finished talking. "I wanna work undercover like my dad!"

"It's not the same for women as it is for men. A chic working undercover has to be a stripper or a girlfriend. Has to have sex, smoke, drink and all kinds of stuff..." O'Neil said with a faraway look in her eyes.

"My dad didn't!" she declared not knowing that he most certainly did. Rohan smoked weed, snorted coke and popped pills when he had to, to make a case.

"OK, well let's go inside," she said pulling in front of the Westchester County gun range. Most cops used the city range in Queens but this was closer to the Bronx.

"Wow!" Megan exclaimed at the wide selection of guns adorning the walls. The sound of gunfire from the range area leaked into the front of the store.

"Nice, huh? But we shooting standard 9 millimeter today," Officer O'Neil said busting her bubble.

She had her own ear and eye protection but had to rent a set for Megan. They bought bullets and targets before stepping out onto the range. Officer O'Neil gave her a brief tutorial of loading the gun and had her repeat it.

"You've done this before?" she dared when she perfected it perfectly on the first try.

"Mm-mm," Megan said shaking her head 'no'. She just paid close attention and followed directions. She did so again when the woman showed her how to aim and squeeze the trigger. Once Officer O'Neil unloaded into a target she reeled it in to show off how it's done.

"See that? All center mass and head. This perp is dead!" she proudly proclaimed. She replaced the target with a fresh one as Megan reloaded the magazine. "OK, let's see what you got."

"Line up dots, breath, squeeze," Megan repeated as she'd been taught and pulled the trigger. One by one she fired all 15 shots into the target. Once the gun locked back unloaded, Officer O'Neil retrieved the target.

"No fucking way!" she exclaimed in amazement. The girl had a tight little group in the center of the target. "Beginners luck! Do it again!"

Megan shrugged and reloaded. Once again she filled the center of the target. Officer O'Neil tried her once more and got the same results.

"Damn, girl! You ready!" the cop proclaimed.

"I sure am," she agreed. They cut it off early since they had a cop funeral to attend in the morning.

Chapter 14

"You OK?" Megan asked and regretted it instantly. Of course she wasn't okay. Her man just got murdered. Her grandmother certainly didn't look okay dressed in all black, rocking back and forth on her bed. The funeral was set to begin soon so she had to say something to get her moving. "It's time, grandma."

"OK," she said somberly and stood. Her knees creaked loudly and her back popped as she became only partially erect. She had aged ten years in the week since her man died.

"Come on, Theo. It's time to go," she said to her brother playing video games.

They weren't officially family so there would be no police escorts or limo ride to the funeral. Instead the second family walked over to the bus station and waited. They didn't have to wait long before one came to a hissing stop in front of them. The bus hissed again and departed towards the train station.

Megan instinctively looked left to the weed spot and saw some guys from her projects. Even the ones who sold weed bought their weed to smoke from here. Grip was front and center talking loud like the leader. His stock had risen from bodying a cop and his brother going away to prison again. He was feeling himself so much he winked at Megan as she rode by and locked eyes. To his surprise she actually winked back. He knew Michelle was her mom so getting his dick in her mouth too would make him the man. Her reputation of being un-fuckable made him decide to make her wifey. He would push up whenever she returned from where ever she was going.

"What's wrong with you?" little Jax asked seeing his sister's face morph into a mask of murder.

"Huh? Nothing. Mind your business, Martin," she said and shook the look away. She was mindful not to engage in their usual bicker so not to upset their grieving grandmother. Dianne stared off into blank space as they switched from bus to train then walked over to the church.

"It's full," a cop announced when they tried to enter. Dianne cocked her head and blinked as if he'd spoken a foreign language.

"We're family," Megan stepped forward and spoke up. With it she officially became the adult of the household.

"Name?" the cop asked, twisting his brow into a question mark as he pulled his clipboard once more. He was pretty sure all family members were checked off and seated.

"Johnson, Dianne," Megan said with a sinking feeling. She wasn't the least bit surprised when he lifted his head back up.

"No Dianne. How are you related?" he asked hoping not to have to turn them away. The silence that followed told him this was his side chick. Not a cop funeral passed that didn't have at least one. Sometimes two and several children.

"I'm his, his..." Dianne finally spoke up then stopped at 'side chick'. Until someone started a 'side chicks matter' movement they would always be off to the side. "Forget it."

"Grandma!" Megan pleaded when her grandmother dropped her head and walked away. She seemed to age another two years just that quickly. That was on the outside but the inside was far worse. She was a broken woman.

*****

Dianne was forced to watch the spectacle of a cop's funeral on the TV. She saw the grieving widow accept the flag with his children and grandchildren seated next to her. Life insurance checks were already deposited in accounts and they were set for life.

Meanwhile Megan watched the activity down in the courtyard. The pack of girls cackled and smoked as their babies stared up from well used, hand-me-down strollers. She tried to focus on them but Grip's annoying voice kept breaking through. He happened to look up and saw Megan staring down at him. It confirmed what he'd been bragging about all day.

"Bitch on my nuts," he repeated for the hundredth time since she winked at him on the bus. He'd been waiting on her to return but missed her when Meka traded him a few minutes worth of pussy in exchange for the blunt she was smoking with the rest of the girls. Of course it was the brown weed they sold instead of the fluffy green stuff they copped a few blocks over they personally smoked.

"She ain't fucking, yo! Err'body tried to hit that," Mook said truthfully. He would know since he shot his best at her just like everyone else in the projects. And just like everyone else, he got shot down. Hers was the holy grail of pussy.

"I'ma fuck her, I bet. You see how fat that ass is?" Grip said gritting his teeth for emphasis. Fat asses tend to make dudes dramatic.

Megan disappeared from the window to tend to her family. She comforted Dianne during her boo's 21-gun salute. She was in need of comfort herself when her grandmother sobbed deep heart wrenching sobs. All she could do was hold her and rock her and tell her she loved her.

"Come on. Go lay down while I cook dinner," Megan said lifting her off the sofa. She escorted her to her room and helped her out of her funeral clothes.

"What am I supposed to do now?" Dianne asked desperately. Megan didn't know but knew that wasn't what she needed to hear.

"Just relax. I'll take care of it. Of you," she said and left the room. She found her brother playing video games as usual. "What you want for dinner, Mike?"

"Hamburgers!" he cheered just like she knew he would. It was the easiest meal to make so she jumped on it.

*****

The apartment was quiet and settled once little Jax and Dianne finally went to sleep. Megan showered, brushed teeth and got in her bed but sleep just wouldn't come. She had long become accustomed to the din of the projects outside but tonight it was amplified. Out of all the noises and chatter, Grip's voice came through above them all.

"Hate you," Megan said when she got in the window and looked down on Grip and his friends. Her grandmother was balled into a fetal position from her grief of losing her man and he was yucking it up with his friends. She watched and listened. Listened and watched for hours until she couldn't take anymore.

"Yo, I'm about to smash your baby mama," Mook said when one of the hood rats winked at him.

"Which one?" Grip asked since he had kids by two of them. Not that he particularly cared, he was just curious. "Let Na-Na get on top or if you fuck Crystal, get that from the back."

"Bet," he said and went over and led Crystal away by her hand. One by one the dope boys carted off one of the hood rats for sex of some kind.

"Shit more money for me!" Grip called out when he became the last man standing. Last dope boy sitting on the bench that is and making all the sales.

Megan was on autopilot when she eased out of her room. She crept into her grandmother's room and over to the night stand. After staring down at her for a full minute she made her move. The heavy old drawer took a good pull to get opened but she got it open it. She blinked curiously at the small vibrator front and center in the drawer. She shrugged and nudged it aside and grabbed what she came for.

She was about to change out of the little shorts and T-shirt she wore around the house but shook the thought out of her head. Instead she removed her bra then tied a knot in the bottom of the shirt to show off her hard stomach. She tugged the shorts up into her crotch to display the plump vagina beneath and set off outside.

"What you tryna cop?" Grip asked a junky who ambled over to his bench. While his partners were busy bouncing up and down in the community coochie, he was getting all the money.

"A dime," the crack-stitute said producing a ten dollar bill she just sucked out some dudes dick. Megan paused in the doorway until the deal was done before making her presence known.

"Psst!" she called out. He darted his eyes in all directions, so she repeated it a few times until he spotted her. "Psst."

"Me?" he asked when she waved him over. Megan 'psst-ed' once more so her voice would not be heard. One thing she knew about the projects was someone was always watching so she stayed out of sight. He hopped up and made a beeline over to her. First he stopped by the bushes to grab his stash and his gun. He was still toting the 32 magnum used to kill the cop. "Knew she was on my nuts!"

"Sup with you?" Megan asked in well rehearsed sexy voice. She'd practiced so much she pulled it off perfectly.

"Shit, you!" he said staring between her legs then up to her nipples. "What you tryna do?"

"It's whatever with me," she said seductively and turned away. The large ass led him up the stairs like a carrot on a stick. The projects roof was dubbed the rooftop motel for kids without cash who wanted to fuck. A good percentage of the projects children were conceived up here. He was so focused on her backside he didn't notice the paper bag in her hand.

"Come here!" Grip said and attacked as soon as they reached the rooftop. He scooped her around her waist and slid his tongue in her mouth. A wave of confusion swept over her when she felt her vagina throb and get wet instantly. She threatened to get swept away in the riptide until she remembered why she was here. Still...

"Let me see your dick?" she dared. The words were barely out of her mouth before the dick was out of his jeans. She slid one hand in the bag but the other reached out to touch it.

"Go on and suck it for me," he urged, cocking his head to the side trying to be sexy. Meanwhile she cocked the gun in the bag and raised it.

"Nah," she declined and fired. Grip dropped so quickly it was as if death snatched him to the ground. She leaned over to get a closer look at her first dead body. He looked sleep except for the neat hole in his forehead. A second later she straightened up and headed for the stairwell. She made sure no one was in the stairwell before running down to her floor. She eased the front door opened and slid inside. She crept back down the hall and listened at her grandmother's door. Hearing nothing she eased in and put the gun back where she found it. She froze when the heavy drawer made a noise when she closed it. Dianne didn't move so she did and crept back out.

Dianne opened her eyes and rolled over to check the drawer she just heard. Megan had no idea how many times her mom got caught sneaking in her drawer growing up.

"Hmm?" she asked seeing her vibrator was moved. She hoped the girl hadn't used it then put it back. The smell of graphite reached her nostril and made her check her gun. A sniff told her it was freshly fired making her frown in confusion. She wasn't sure what just happened so she wiped it free of prints and put it back.

*****

"What's going on out there?" Megan asked when she came out into the living room. She'd seen the heavy police presence from her window and already knew.

"They found another dead body!" little Jax exclaimed almost cheerfully. These projects were all he knew so he was immune to death already.

"Who?" Megan asked making her grandmother twist her lips. She had already gotten the call about the rare gun being found on the dead guy and the case was as good as closed. There would be no investigation as to who killed this piece of shit.

"Some boy called Grip. You know him?" she asked knowingly. The report of a single bullet to the forehead matched the single bullet missing from her gun.

"Grip? Grip... I don't know... uh oh!" she exclaimed when her lie was interrupted by a knock on the door. She just knew it was the police coming to lock her up. She would probably have to share a cell with her mother.

"Who?" Dianne asked through the door. The muffled reply made her look through the peephole before pulling it open for the courier.

"Dianne Johnson?" he asked from the name on the envelope. She nodded her head up and down so he pushed his clipboard forward. "Sign here."

Dianne signed curiously and thanked him. Once she closed the door behind him she opened the envelope. Her frowned deepened then flipped upside down.

"What, grandma?" Megan asked. She was relieved it wasn't the police but something had her grandmother elated. Dianne was too happy for speech so she handed the content over.

Megan smiled too at the life insurance check for twenty five thousand dollars. It was a drop in the bucket compared to what his family got but Officer Johnson still looked out for his baby.

Chapter 15

Twenty five thousand dollars is like a million dollars to poor people. My brother didn't know we were poor because this was all he knew. Me, I knew the difference between a middle class home in the suburbs and the projects. Still, my grandmother stretched that money as far as money has ever been stretched before in history. Our lifestyle didn't change much; she just augmented it, plus an etcetera or two. It lasted almost a full year. Good thing it ran out when it did because it was time for my mother to come home.

"Sup, yo!" Megan greeted the girls on the bench. One had moved on when her parents moved down south but two younger ones quickly replaced her. They recently came of age and had babies as a right of passage. Now they too could ride that bench and brag about how bad their baby is.

"Sup, Megan!" they all called out making sure to call her by name. She was almost a role model to the girls who accepted life in the projects. They were headed nowhere in life but knew her time with them was limited. At least when she popped up famous they could say they knew her.

Megan stifled a smirk as she looked over to the dope boys' bench minus Grip. Not a day went by that she didn't think of the deed that left him dead and smile. It was justice and justice feels good. Mook got to be the man for a full two weeks until someone killed him in a robbery. Alex moved up and took his spot with Young P waiting on his demise so he could move up. Hem wasn't just waiting. He was plotting because no one really wants to be in second place, or a runner up.

All eyes switched to her switching ass as she passed by on her way home. It seems like it had gotten fatter with every day that went by. The senior was pretty as a picture and fine and the proverbial 'mother fucker'. She got a kick out of men's and some women's reaction to her. Most of her lady swag was courtesy of Officer O'Neil but no one in the projects or school knew the woman.

Angel called from time to time to kick it but Megan refused to go anywhere with her ever again. She forgave her after the hard luck story of letting Rico and Walt run a train on her. Rico let all his friends fuck her until she came up pregnant. Their weary grandmother finally gave up and sent her to Atlanta to live with her father.

Megan felt an odd feeling when she entered her building. It slowed her pace as she tried to figure it out. Except for when she reached the pissy steps. She took a breath and sprinted up to her floor. She confirmed something was off when she didn't hear her little brother as she approached the door. Usually he could be heard down the hall shouting along to his video games.

"Megan!" Jax shouted and slammed into her as she as she opened the door. She looked down curiously, wondering what had gotten into him. It was explained when she heard her name called.

"Megan? Oh my God! Look at you!" Michelle exclaimed and threw her arms open. This was the same warm reunion that scared the wits out of her little brother since he didn't know the woman claiming to be his mother.

"Look at you," Megan said with far more venom than even she expected. A pleading look from her grandmother softened her tone. "I mean, look at you! You look good."

Michelle did indeed look good after five years of being clean and sober. She looked a lot better than Reese did running around the projects sucking dicks and doing assorted tricks to get high. Michelle had her weight back, her hair was shiny and strong and her skin was clear.

"Your mother has a job already! She gonna be working at the A and P!" Dianne cheered as if the supermarket was IBM. It was better than being in jail and far better than being a crack head.

"Yeah my P.O. says I gotta keep a job," Michelle explained. She still had ten years on paper and had to keep her nose clean.

"Who is she?" Jax whispered up to his sister. He wasn't buying some strange woman popping in, out the blue claiming to be his mother.

"That's Michelle, Garry," she said looking her in her eyes. "She's our mom."

"So where's our dad?" he asked since it was finally being talked about. He'd always gotten shut up or shut down when he asked questions but this time they bought this to him.

"Dead," Megan said daring her mother to say otherwise. Michelle just poked out her bottom lip and nodded in surrender.

"I'm not mad. I can't be. All I ask is a chance to be a mom?" Michelle pleaded. Her mother nodded hopefully from the background hoping they could all be a family again.

"So, where you staying? Cuz the house..." Megan asked and jabbed. She still had nightmares about what happened to her home on Long Island. Seeing it gutted like that haunted her.

"Here, but you guys can keep my room. I'll take the sofa," she explained.

"It'll be fine. Just fine, watch and see!" Dianne cheered because she had to. She had to hope and believe everything would be okay. Jail can change hardened men into soft women so maybe it could change this hardened woman into one as well.

*****

"Soooo, how's 12th grade?" Officer O'Neil asked as she and Megan circled each other in the ring. Megan was an exceptional boxer so she took advantage of the question and threw a jab.

"How I knew you was going to do that!" Megan laughed and slipped under the punch.

"So far so good. My mom, too. Works and sleeps."

"That's what's, up," Officer O'Neil said along with a combination. Megan bobbed and weaved that one and the one after it. It was to the point where she couldn't hit the girl anymore.

"How's work?" Megan shot back with a two-piece. Officer O'Neal dipped the first blow but got knocked back a few steps by the second one. "Oops, sorry!"

"For what?" she asked and threw a body blow, followed by an uppercut. Megan rolled away and ducked the blows. "Never say or do shit you don't mean and you'll never have be sorry."

"OK," she said, adding the lesson to all the others. She kept them on reserve for later use, later in life. "Can we go shooting?"

"Sure," she agreed since she wasn't getting anywhere with her in the ring. They wrapped it up at the next bell and hit the locker. As usual she made small talked while they undressed, and showered. As usual she saw the girl looking her over. This time she asked, "You got a boyfriend?"

"Huh?" she asked looking up from her ass. "No! Why? Who said I did?"

"You like girls?" Officer O'Neil asked and faced her for a reply. She got a mixed answer when the girl glanced down at her twat then up to reply.

"No! I don't have time for boys and their games and a girl! Eww!" she said believably enough for her to believe her. She obviously just liked looking at pretty women. Officer O'Neil could relate since she appreciated pretty women too without wanting to be with one. They finished up in the gym and headed up to Westchester to the range.

*****

"You wanna grab a drink or something?" Michelle asked her pretty coworker, Tina, when closing time came. A recovering junky has no business drinking but she needed an excuse to hang out with the pretty woman.

"Um, I don't really drink, but OK, I guess?" Tina guessed. She liked the older lady but not in the way Michelle liked her.

Michelle kept a girlfriend the whole time she was in prison and developed a taste for vagina. Especially dark chocolate ones like the one this pretty black girl had to have under that skirt. The two kicked it all day at adjacent registers and got cool. It was payday so why not hang out for a little while before going home.

"I don't really drink either but..." Michelle said and paused when she couldn't find a valid excuse. She had been doing well since coming home and the kids were coming around. Megan was still slightly standoffish, but that was part of her personality. Little Jax allowed her play videos games with him. She won that one by default since neither Megan nor Dianne would play the violent games with him.

Michelle cashed her check at lunchtime and separated her meager earnings. She divided it into four different pockets in her purse. One was for her mom to help around the house. Two were for her kids and their kid stuff. Last and the least was a couple of twenty-dollar bills for her own bus and lunch fare.

She decided she would have to skip a couple days lunch to take the girl out. If she had her way she'd be eating Tina's pussy for lunch, dinner and desert.

"I always wanted to stop in here!" Tina admitted as Michelle led her into a nearby sports bar. Michelle mentally pumped her fist since she scored a point by taken her somewhere she's never been.

"Well, fuck with me and I'll take you plenty of places you never been," Michelle bragged. Tina cocked her head curiously then shrugged if off. They found a spot at the crowded bar and squeezed in.

"Cheers," Tina cheered when they received their super strong, fruity drinks. They clinked glasses and sipped.

"Mph!" Michelle reeled when she tasted the alcohol. It awakened something that had been dormant inside for the years away. She could almost hear, and feel it stirring inside.

"It is good!" Tina giggled with some of the concoction on her top lip. It looked too good to pass up so Michelle made her move. Tina froze when she leaned in and sucked the drink from her lip. Michelle mistook her lack of protest and upped the ante by sticking her tongue in her mouth. Tina suddenly came to life and pushed away.

"What?" Michelle asked, confused by the shocked look on her face. The patrons around all paused to see what was coming next.

"What? You kissed me is what! I'm not fucking gay!" she shouted in her face. She remembered the drink in her hand and doused her with it before storming off.

"She bugging. Heh, heh," Michelle chuckled and told the shocked onlookers. She turned back to her drink and took a sip. Then a guzzle and finally downed it. She had one more before taking a cab home. By the time she reached the projects she had a good buzz going and had spent most of her weekly allotment.

She tried to ignore the dope boys as she walked briskly through the courtyard. The temptation was always there but she always ignored it. Her addiction buzzed around her ears like a pesky, persistent housefly begging for attention. Seeing the state Reese was in was a helluva motivator not to fuck around but tonight's rejection made her weak and vulnerable and...

"You got a nick?" she asked ready to part with her last five. She would just have a little blast from the past and go to bed.

"Here you go, ma," a young boy said as he served her. He was too young to remember her before she went away and had no problem selling her dope.

"First things first," Michelle chided herself as she rushed upstairs. Everyone was sleeping so she went into her mother's room and woke her up. "Ma, take y'all money!"

"No, baby!" Dianne wailed at the familiar look in her eyes.

"No, baby, what? I'm giving you my money so I wont get into nothing!" she swore.

Dianne took the money with a lonely sigh. "I'm about to take my shower and go to bed."

That was half the true but the straight shooter she'd hidden years ago was still in the vent. She pulled it free and took a long, deep sizzling hit. And once again, it's on!

Chapter 16

Mitchell fought the power for as long as she possibly could. She resisted using again after her brief relapse for a full month. Tina wouldn't speak with her, Megan was busy with her life and her son just wanted to play video games.

"Everybody got their thing so what about me? I don't get to have a thing?" she asked aloud as she climbed the hill towards home. It was payday and she had her whole check in her purse. "Shit, I get to have something! I deserve it!"

'Get high. You do deserve it!' the devil urged in his trademark whisper. Michelle nodded in agreement and picked up her pace until she was marching like a North Korean soldier.

Megan just happened to be in the window when her mother entered the courtyard. She could tell by her walk that something was off. She didn't get a chance to wonder what, because she was headed straight for the dope boys.

"Welp, that's the end of that," she shrugged when she watched the drug deal. By now she could spot deal or dealer from a mile away. She could tell if someone was carrying a gun just by their walk. A look in the eye could spot a criminal in an instant. Her years of people watching would help her when she became a cop.

"Shit better be butter," Michelle warned as she inspected the two dime sized rocks in her palm. They should be enough to take the edge off so she could get back to regular life. All she needed was some relief.

"You look like you butter!" Young P proclaimed, looking her up and down. All the dope boys fuck all the dope fiends at one point or another. Usually late at night when nothing is happening. At least until they shrivel down to nothing but bones with the trademark big head. This was a new one so he wanted to be first inside her. New to him since she'd been fucking around these projects before he was born.

"Yeah it is for the right bread," she quipped and laughed at her own joke. She put a little extra in her walk as she walked away since she knew her ass cheeks had an audience.

"I'ma smash that!" Young P nodded and grabbed his young manhood through his jeans.

"She on the dope. We all gonna smash that," another corrected.

"Shit, shit," Michelle fussed when she reached her building. The first shit was because she realized she couldn't smoke in the apartment with everyone up and about. The second shit was at the loss of her second option since Reese no longer had an apartment.

Reese lived in the rooftop motel during warmer weather, then got in where she could during the cold New York fall and winters. Cracks heads are the strongest creatures on the planet able to withstand the tremendous abuse they subjected their selves to.

First was the intense heat of crack smoke they ingested daily all day. Then the beatings they could withstand from constant stealing and scheming. Then there were all those dicks, fucking and sucking all day and all night in exchange for dope. Then oral, anal, vaginal or any other freaky way someone could come up with. She spotted a known smoker copping rocks and followed her into the next building.

"Sup, Eloise. Let me use your shooter," she asked cordially. Gone were the days of borrowing a cup of sugar. She was in search of a crack pipe.

"You got dope?" Eloise demanded. It cost to ride the bus, train or taxicab so she certainly wasn't riding on her pipe for free. She would have to pay to get where she was trying to go.

"Just a dime. I'll split it with you," she bargained and followed her up to her shell of an apartment. It had been smoked clean of all valuables like electronics and family.

"Me first!" the host demanded and stuck out a weathered monkey paw. She watched carefully as Michelle split her rock in 'half' and handed it over. Michelle watched just as closely as she sucked the dope down the stem. An unholy alliance between two crack heads was formed.

*****

Another alliance was being formed as well. It had actually been years in the making as a couple of nerdy teens smiled and blinked in high school hallways. One finally got up the nerve to say something to the other.

"Sup, yo," Megan said unsure which persona to use with him. "I'm Megan."

"Um, Gerald," he said formally and extended his hand. She squinted at it for a second before reaching out and giving it a shake. He was a pretty, dark young man, oblivious to how he affected women. His math teacher liked to cross her legs and squeeze and release while staring at him until she bust on herself.

"That's my little brother's name," she replied since she called him it just that morning. She was still on a roll and never once called him by his given name or by any of the names she'd given, more than once.

"I see you're a senior too?" he asked even though he knew she was. They traded small talk back and forth until the bell separated them. They traded phone numbers and departed.

Gerald and Megan talked daily, then day and night for weeks until he worked up the nerve to ask her out. When he suggested they go down to 42nd street her mind flashed to Angel giving Rico a hand job and blushed.

"Or not..." he said nervously when she went silent on the phone from the memory.

"Oh, no! I mean yes! Sure, I was just, um... sure! When?" she stammered trying to fix it. The date was set so she quickly hung up before she said something stupid. Something else, stupid that is.

"Yo Megan, let me hold ten bucks 'til I get paid tomorrow?" Michelle asked when her daughter emerged from the rear.

"I wish I would," she huffed indignantly at the request. She'd seen her mother buying drugs on several occasions since she fell off the wagon and had no desire to waste her little allowance on her.

"You really got a smart mouth. Don't make me put my hands on you," she said puffing herself up. Michelle had a mean fight game honed in these same projects and perfected upstate in prison.

"I wish you would," Megan laughed and took a boxers stand without putting her hands up. She was going to respect the bond of motherhood until the woman put her hands on her or her brother. Michelle peeped her stance and knew the girl knew what she was doing. It was more trouble than she wanted so she relented. There's more than one way to skin a cat so she set out to explore them.

*****

"Sup, yo. Let me get a couple dimes until tomorrow. I get paid tomorrow and I been spending real good with you all week," Michelle laid out her spiel as she walked down the stairs. It sounded reasonable so she nodded and went to try it out. "Yo, P. Let me holla at you real quick."

"Told y'all niggers!" he said to his partners before going over since he was pretty sure what she wanted. Had it been a drug deal she would have came and copped like she'd been doing all week. She hadn't been smoking long enough this time to lose that fat ass she'd been slinging around when she walked. "Sup, ma?"

"You. Check it, I been spending real good and..." she began her well rehearsed appeal but Young P cut in and cut to the chase.

"I'm trying to fuck something. What's happening?" he insisted. "I'll throw you something once we done."

"How much?" she demanded indignantly. It was common knowledge that Reese was running around selling two dollar blow jobs and no way was she selling herself that short.

"Shit..." he paused to ponder since none of his peers popped her pussy yet. Being first had value so he offered, "I'll give you a couple twenties."

"Run it!" she agreed for a couple reasons. First and foremost she wanted to get high. Second, she hadn't had any dick in over five years and felt moisture creeping into her panties as she looked the solid teen up and down. She developed a taste for vagina while she was away but couldn't come up on any of that either. "Where we going?"

"Shit, we can go to my spot!" he said adamantly as if it really was his spot. He stayed with his grandmother but a few forties of malt liquor a day allowed him carte blanche to do whatever he wanted.

He reached out and palmed her ass as they entered his building. His elevator happened to be working that day so they rode up to the top floor. He led her down the hall, into the apartment.

"Need another one," the old lady inside said holding up a almost empty forty ounce bottle.

"Hmp," he said parting with two dollars. The woman accepted it and stood without ever even looking at Michelle. Young P pulled her down the hallway and into his room. "Take all your clothes off. Socks too!"

Michelle laughed knowing where he was coming from. Girls his age were girls his age and any woman he'd been with her age didn't look anything like she did. She was full grown and fine, so he planned to enjoy this.

"May have to charge you extra," she said patting his nice sized dick when it came out. It was so hard and ready it quivered like a diving board. She knew then he planned to beat the pussy up and that was just fine by her.

"Bet," he agreed for another twenty when he seen what was under her clothes as well.

"Yo, don't tell nobody about this..."

"About wha... oh, OK. Ssss," she asked, answered and hissed when he dipped down and licked some of that grown lady pussy. Michelle kept a tidy box and the teen went to town sucking and licking on it. It didn't take long until she bust a nut in his mouth. She reached down and grabbed him by his dick to pull him up. She cocked her legs wide and slipped him inside.

Young P took a few exploratory strokes until he got his bearings, then went to town. He scooped her thick thighs under his arms and bent her in half. She wiggled and squirmed under his relentless, young boy stroke. The kid had one speed and one motion like a Texas oil rig. Just like that oil rig he hit a gusher as she came over and over. Twenty minutes later he seized up and bust a nut of his own inside of her.

"Shit! You, got some, good, pussy!" he proclaimed in the process of catching his breath. She made it harder to catch by squeezing his sensitive dick with her vagina.

"Yup, sure do and you can get it whenever you want it," she assured him.

"I can?" he asked dumbfounded. "Oh yeah, cuz I'm paying, huh?"

"Well that too," she said since she was complimenting him fucking her so well. Still he broke her off and she went off to get high. She had her own pipe and spring, so she no longer needed Eloise.

Chapter 17

"Who?" Megan called out even though she was pretty sure who it should be.

She used the extra seconds to check her appearance once more. It was good timing since her mother wasn't in one of her cracked out comas. Michelle could go hard for a few days, then had to shut down for a day. She was smoking real good now after Young P bragged about how good the pussy was. Now all the dope boys were throwing dope at her to make love to her. She was smoking so good she no longer needed her job. That was only for parole anyway and she fucked that up when she started smoking again.

"Um, me. Um, Gerald," Gerald remembered after a momentary brain freeze. The six foot two inch nerd had the body of an athlete, face of an angel and the social grace of a turtle. He used his thick glasses to hide behind just like a turtle does its shell.

"Hey," she sang, blushed and swayed when she opened the door halfway.

"Let him in!" Dianne fussed from the sofa. She wanted a look at whoever got the girl to finally go on a date. "Mmm, chocolate."

"Don't mind my grandmother. She's crazy," Megan explained as little Jax came to investigate as well. "And this is my brother, Fernando."

"I thought you said?" he asked remembering her telling him they shared the same name. Jax just looked him up and down to check him out and went back to the back and his game.

"Where you taking my baby?" Dianne asked twisting her lips at Megan's below the knee dress. She couldn't recall ever seeing her wear one. It wasn't anywhere near as short as the one Angel wore the night they went out but the intent was the same. He could touch her if he wanted to since they now went together. This was the first time they actually went anywhere together but made it official a week ago.

"To the movies. I wanted to see Spider Man but she insist on Yolo," he sighed rehashing their running debate.

"Yolo! I been wanting to see that my damn self! Let me get my purse!" she exclaimed and stood. Gerald smiled and nodded at the suggestion but Megan wasn't having it. She wanted to experience whatever feeling had Angel's eyes fluttering in the movie theatre.

"How 'bout, no," Megan laughed knowing she was goofing around. "I'll be home in a few."

"I know you will," Dianne smiled and nodded. She had gotten a do-over raising her grandkids and did a damn good job. She accepted defeat with her fucked up daughter but these were some good kids. Life rarely gives do-overs and she made the best of it.

*****

"Bruh, hurry up," Monte fussed as Steve made love to Michelle. They were supposed to be running a train but here he was tongue kissing and slow grinding. A win win for Michelle who enjoyed the sex as well and the dope they paid her. She was still fine enough to charge a premium for pussy. Once it loses it's elasticity the value would drop substantially. Reese couldn't pay anyone to fuck her now. She was regulated to washing cars and running errands for her daily dope.

"Mmm, get this pussy," Michelle purred and grinded back. Life was good since all she did was screw and smoke. She let out a soft whimper and had a hard orgasm.

"Come on, yo!" Monte fussed again hearing her moan in pleasure. The pussy was so wet it was squishing and squelching loudly.

"Argh! Whew! Shit, this some good pussy!" Steve announced like an official proclamation and came in it. It was even wetter now since he pumped her full of teen come.

"Move!" Monte demanded and pulled him away. He plunged inside a second later and went to humping. "Damn, this shit is wet!"

Michelle noticed the change in dick size and squeezed to accommodate the smaller one. The teen still had a good stroke and started feeling good. She grabbed his hips and helped slam him in and out, up and down. It was a race to get off before he did but she lost two minutes later.

"Ugh! Shit! Yeah!" Monte cheered as he added to the collection of cum in the woman. She now had three different donations in her vagina and two in her stomach. The night was still young so she would more than likely add to it.

*****

"I've never been down here," Gerald admitted as they emerged from the subway at Times Square. He was too busy with school and college prep to hang out downtown.

"Well I'll show you around," Megan offered and took him by his hand. She was a vet since she'd been here once before. Gerald let out a goofy giggle when she held his hand as they strolled along. "I wonder what's in here?"

"You do?" he asked as she led him into the sex shop. The dildos in the window told him what it was but he was with her and followed her inside.

"Oh wow!" they both exclaimed as a new world of freakiness opened up for them both. Their mouths hung open at the display of dicks being sucked and vaginas being licked. They perused through the stacks of DVDs of all kinds of fucking.

"Um, OK," Megan said, having seen enough. She led the way back out onto the sidewalk. They took hands again and set back off to the theatre.

"Glad I got tickets online!" he said, seeing the long line out front. They bypassed it and walked inside through the express line. Gerald bought everything Megan pointed at in the concession stand and they went inside.

They made small talk until the lights went dim. She spread her legs ever so slightly just in case he wanted to play in her pussy like Rico and Angel. She would return the favor if he did. She shook her head at the fitted cap in front of them and laughed.

"What?" Gerald asked of her chuckle since the movie hadn't started yet.

"Nothing," she giggled again and scooted closer. She giggled again when he put his arm around her. Her legs parted a little more but it wasn't to be. He actually was here to see the movie.

"Ooh! Oh wow!" Gerald cheered as Yolo went wild on the big screen. Megan was slightly disappointed at not being touched, but the Lovely Little Lunatic made up for it.

They were still gushing about it when they rode the train back uptown. He had money for a taxi but they decided to walk so they could have extra time together. Their fingers interlocked and swung as they strolled along. They play fought, kicking and punching as they reenacted some of the movie. The walk ended far to quickly and they reached the projects far sooner than they wanted to.

"He with me!" Megan told a group of goons lurking in the darkness. They would have robbed Gerald on the way out without the disclaimer.

"Bet," one said, granting him a 'get out of the projects free pass'. They went back to wait on other prey.

Megan hoped her crazy mother didn't pop out from somewhere and embarrass her. She'd walked in on her giving a blow job in the stairwell once and prayed tonight wouldn't be twice. She let out a sigh of relief when they found it empty except the pissy aroma. They held their breath and took the steps by twos.

"Well, thank you. I had fun," Megan said coyly when they reached her door.

"Yeah, me too. I um," he replied before Megan leaned up and kissed him. Shoved her tongue in his mouth actually. He wrapped his strong arms around her and joined the kiss.

Megan felt his erection pop up so quick it pushed her back slightly. She leaned against him and kept kissing. She was so into the kiss she didn't hear the door open behind her.

"That's plenty!" Dianne said snatching Megan away and inside.

"Bye!" she called out sounding love sick as her grandmother closed the door on her date. "Grandma!"

"Don't grandma me! I ain't ready to be no great grandma!" she fussed putting the locks on the door. Megan blushed so hard Dianne realized she wasn't having sex yet. But sucking face with a boy is how it starts so she stopped it.

Meanwhile outside Gerald was blushing and giggling about his first make out session ever. He was a little lightheaded from the erection as he headed towards the stairwell. A woman was coming up as he headed down and they met in the middle of the steps.

"Want your dick sucked?" she asked, pointing a finger at him. Gerald paused to analyze the seemingly rhetorical question.

On the surface the answer would be yes. Yes, he did want his dick sucked since everyone with a dick wants it sucked. But she obviously meant now and by her, so that would be a no.

"No, thank you," he replied to the offer and resumed on his way. Michelle shrugged the rejection off and headed up to the apartment.

"Here come one... oh, that's Megan people," one of the stick up boys said as Gerald approached. He used his pass and passed safely out of the projects.

"Well, I'm going to bed," Megan announced when her mother walked in. She'd lost the trace of respect she had for the woman when she started smoking again.

"So," Michelle quipped behind her back as she walked off. She was hood enough to see her daughter was about that life even if she was still a nerd. All the dope boys were caught up with their teen girlfriends leaving her without a trick to treat. She still wanted to get high and looked around for something of value. Nothing was present except her son's last birthday present. It had value.

"Wonder why she was all, 'ooh' and 'sss'?'" Megan said as she recalled Angel's reaction to Rico's touch that night. She wondered and slid her hand under her sleep shirt and into her panties. Her vagina was wet when she reached it so she slid a finger around her slippery lips. She inadvertently touched her clit and found out what the 'sss' was about. "Sss! Mmm."

Megan explored her wet vagina like a new toy. She slightly inserted a finger then withdrew to focus on her throbbing clitoris. A band started playing off in the distance as the feeling grew and radiated. She could feel Gerald's tongue in her mouth and arms wrapped around her as the band took it to the bridge. They reached their crescendo just as she reached her first climax.

"Shit, Gerald!" she shouted, blaming busting this nut on him. She shivered and shook unaware of just how loud she was until she heard her brother's snickers.

"What you doing?" he asked when her head snapped in his direction. He was too young to know what just happened.

"Minding my damn business! Go to sleep!" she fussed in embarrassment. Luckily for her he did go back to sleep quickly and she went for round two.

Chapter 18

"What?" Megan asked as her brother searched frantically through the house. Dianne already knew the deal when he first asked about his game. It was the latest system with all the bells and whistles, but it didn't have legs so they knew it didn't walk up out of the apartment on its own.

"I can't find my game?" he said checking under the bed, in the closet and finally under his pillow. Megan blew a fuse and stormed up to the living room.

"Where is she?" she demanded when she didn't see the 'lump on the log' as she referred to her mother sleep on the sofa.

"What's wrong?" her grandmother asked as if she didn't already know. She stole from herself to know her daughter stole from her own son.

"That bitch stole Nate's games!" she growled and checked the kitchen. "Bruh, when I catch her I'm gonna beat her ass! Harvey loved his damn game."

"Maybe she didn't um, or um... shit, she took it," Dianne sighed. She tried her best to treat her daughter like family but her daughter chose the streets over her family. She wanted to calm her grandchild so she wouldn't put her hands on her mother but a knock on the door forced her to press pause. Megan ran over and snatched the door open so violently both guest pulled their guns.

"Michelle Robinson?" the first cop asked from behind his gun. He scanned the room before stepping fully inside.

"That's not her. Where's Michelle?" the probation officer asked in a softer tone as she lowered her weapon.

"In the streets," Dianne said, finally accepting that that's where she was happy. That's where she wanted to be and that's where she belonged. Where she lived and most likely where she would die.

"Well she missed her last few appointments with me. I've tried to spare her since she has so much time left on paper," the woman appealed. She was hoping the family would vouch for her and vow to bring her in as soon as possible. Drug addicts need programs, not prison but the judge promised to send her back for the rest of her ten years if she blew probation.

"That's cuz she too busy to come down," Megan offered. "Too busy smoking crack, turning tricks and stealing out our house!"

"Who are you?" the probation officer asked, cocking her head to get a better look.

"She gave birth to me 18 years ago," she replied, rounding up to her next birthday. Technically she had a few more months until she turned eighteen but already had plans. No roller skating, no clubs, she was taking the test to become a New York City police officer.

"Wow, OK. Um, well tell her she needs to report," she said and mentally wrote her off. If her own family couldn't support her, why should she? She left her card and left the apartment and projects off to her next adult delinquent.

"And just where are you going?" Dianne demanded when Megan put her play sneakers on and went for the door.

"To find Michelle so I can get Donald's game back!" she huffed. Dianne pursed her lips at the futile notion. The game was smoked and would have to be replaced.

"Baby, I'll get him a new one. I'll... " she pleaded to prevent her from laying hands on her mother even though she really wanted to beat the woman herself.

"With what? We broke! We don't have money but we have each other and this bitch violated us!" Megan demanded. Her grandmother opened her mouth to reply but found no words. Just a deep sigh at what had to be done.

"Let me get my sneakers," she said and went to do just that. She returned a few minutes later with them laced tightly and VASELINE smeared on her face. "Let's go."

*****

Michelle's mouth was too stuffed with dick to speak so she sighed at the long line waiting to get inside of her. They don't call it a train for nothing she thought to herself. She had one teen in her mouth and one humping away behind her. There were four more sitting around playing video games waiting on their turn.

The novelty of new pussy wore off so now she could only get a twenty rock to get someone's rocks off. Six twenty rocks would last most of the day. She might have to turn a late night trick and suck some late night dick to get through the night. If she was lucky she could stash a 'wake me up' blast for the next morning. The first two got off and got off so the next two could get on and get off.

"Hole up! Smoke break!" Michelle called a crack head time out. She broke a piece off one of the rocks she just got and took a long sizzling pull.

"You better back up, son! Keep breathing that shit and you gone fuck around and be on the pipe too!" one teen warned another.

"Niggas gone be running trains on you!" another one added, cracking them all up except Michelle that is. She was too busy holding the smoke in her lungs. The train resumed its journey as soon as she exhaled a plume of putrid crack smoke. One entered her mouth the other between her legs. The miles were starting to add up on her vagina and she would be washing cars along Reese soon.

The train pulled into the last station and everyone got off. Michelle wisely wore a pad to sop up the semen soup left inside her and got dressed. The warm weather meant she could go up to the roof to smoke so she wouldn't have to share with Eloise.

Michelle had a few dollars in tips so she ambled over to the bodega for a crack head starter kit consisting a forty-ounce malt liquor, menthols and a fresh lighter. She breezed back through the projects and up to the roof.

"Excuse me while I kiss the sky... " Michelle sang as she exited on to the roof. Her song was cut short when she realized she wasn't alone. "What y'all doing up here?"

"You stole Daniel's game?" Megan growled and confronted her.

"You mean Jax who I named after his dick slinging daddy? Shole did and I smoked that shit!" she laughed.

It's said that he who laughs last, laughs best but not today. Today Megan socked her mother in her jaw so hard it spun her around. Dianne was right there to spin her around again. Grandmother and granddaughter beat the deadbeat mother back and forth like a good volley ball at a tennis match. Reese came out on the roof to smoke the piece of rock she earned and saw the beating. She spun on her heels and got out of there.

"And, you, still ain't, getting, the game, back," Michelle taunted as she got her ass whipped. She was knotted and bloody but still laughing and talking shit.

"This shit funny?" Megan asked and suddenly stopped punching. Her face contorted and she ran over and grabbed her mother by her pants.

"No!" Dianne shouted as she ran the woman towards the edge of the roof to toss over. She'd seen many go over the ledge in her decades in these projects. It's never pretty when they reach the ground below. No matter how they looked when they fall, they all look the same when they land.

"I, have, to!" Megan insisted as her grandmother grabbed her before she could throw her over. While they wrestled over the crack head she slipped free and got away. "Dang, grandma!"

"Let her kill herself. You don't need that on your hands, baby. On your soul," Dianne urged. Megan agreed and broke down into sobs for the first time in a long time.

*****

"What?" Gerald asked, seeing Megan was staring off into space instead of watching TV. They went to movies and out to eat occasionally but most times stayed up late watching TV after Jax and Dianne went to bed.

"Huh? Oh, yeah I'm good," she assured him and kissed him to prove it. Most of their late night TV watching sessions turned into late night make out sessions. They would kiss and grope until their tongues went numb but never went past second base. Until tonight that is.

"Wow!" Gerald cheered when she took his hand and guided it between her legs. She masturbated quite often and set him up just how she liked to be touched. "It's so wet!"

"Well, it's a vagina so... " she quipped. She ran out of smart shit to say when his fingers ran circles around her swollen clit. Her legs spread even wider so he could get to it. He misunderstood which led to a misunderstanding. "Chill! Don't put your finger in it!"

"My bad," he apologized and went back to how she showed him how she liked it. Once he got it she leaned up and kissed him once more. Their tongues danced in each other's mouth when she bust a nut in his hand. She clamped her mouth down on his shoulder to muffle her screams and squeals.

"Shit! I mean shoot that felt good!" she exclaimed when her breathing went back to normal. "Want me to do you?"

"Me? I don't have a vagina? Oh wait, you mean... " he stammered and stuttered. Megan pressed her lips together and shook her head. She unzipped his jeans and went in.

"I can't, get, it out!" she said struggling to get his rock hard erection out of the hole. She unbuckled his pants and set it free. "Oh my!"

"What?" he asked wondering if he did something wrong. "What's wrong?"

"Nothing, at, all!" she assured him tugging on his nice, thick dick. As much as she enjoyed it in her hand she had no desire to have it inside of her. Both kids agreed to wait until they married before going all the way. Neither was particularly religious but both seen the ill affects and effects of teen sex. They had a plan for the future that didn't include kids just yet. She was going to be chief of police and him, a lawyer, district attorney and then judge. Neither had any desire to be a baby mama or baby daddy now or ever.

"I um, I mean... " Gerald said looking around. He usually had some tissue when he did this to himself but Megan didn't plan ahead. "Ugh!"

"Wow!" Megan marveled as he erupted and skeeted high in the air. Spurts of cum spewed and spit all over the place. Luckily her grandmother still had the thick plastic covers the sofa came with when she bought it decades ago. Her dress and his pants, however, didn't fare so well.

"My bad," he said, seeing semen everywhere but he felt too good to feel bad.

"Don't worry. I got it," she said and got up. She returned a second later with washcloths to clean him and the sofa. They shared a few more kisses before it was time to go.

"I'll call you when I get in," he assured her with a parting kiss and departed. He called when he got home but didn't get an answer because Megan fell asleep right there on the sofa before he even made it out of the projects.

Chapter 19

This part I like, Candy thought to herself when Cortez slid down between her thick caramel thighs. He made a blasphemous prayer and crossed himself as a joke before he began to eat. Playing hard to get got her exactly what she wanted, inside the dope boy's main house. While other thots threw pussy and blow jobs his way, she remained aloof.

That got the thots fucked in motels and back seats while he wined and dined Candy for months. He bragged about his whole operation the whole way. The harder a woman makes a man work for the pussy, the harder he will work to get that pussy. He lavished the pretty lady with expensive gifts and fed her expensive foods. She forced him to cut off all his women and take her to his main house, instead of one of his many apartments where he screwed his jump offs. He finally got this pussy and was making the best of it.

He twirled his tongue around her pearl tongue until he had her squirming. She glanced at the clock, door and down to the top of his head.

"Shit!" Candy fussed and busted a gushing nut in his mouth. He kept right on sucking and licking in search of another orgasm.

This the part I hate Candy grumbled internally as Cortez did an acrobatic flip into a 69 with him on top. His rock hard dick pressed against her lips, which was bad, but the heavy nut sack laying on her eyes was worse. Even worse was the hairy anus on her forehead. She took another glance at the clock, then door as he pressed his dick into her lips.

"Suck that shit, mama!" he groaned when he finally entered her hot mouth. She didn't get a chance to suck it even if she wanted to because he humped her face like he was in a vagina. He worked his hips up, down and around as he made love to her mouth.

Candy hated being put in this position even though she usually enjoyed a good 69. Hate it or not, Cortez could suck a pussy like a pro.

Her thoughts were interrupted as another orgasm crept up on her. It was more intense than the first but she didn't get to enjoy it.

"Argh! Shit! Take it!" Cortez shouted as he exploded in her mouth. He pressed his dick on her esophagus and filled her mouth with salty semen. She fought not to swallow but had no choice as he literally came down her throat.

He didn't quite get to enjoy it much either when his front door was violently knocked off its hinges. The back door met the same fate and the house quickly filled with masked gunmen. Candy pushed his dick from her mouth and rolled away.

"What the fuck... " Cortez shouted in confusion. He looked towards his gun on the nightstand and calculated his chances.

"Police! Freeze!" the lead cop shouted aiming a red dot of his forehead.

"I wish you would!" another dared as he followed his eyes to the gun. Cortez thought about all the money and drugs in the house and decided to go for it. Luckily for him Candy snatched the gun away before he could make his move. The cops laser sights may have been trained on Cortez but all eyes roamed the woman's voluptuous body.

"Damn, O'Neil! I had no idea you was that fucking fine!" one said, what the rest were thinking.

"Whatever!" she shot back and scrambled for her clothing. She snatched her garments and rushed into the bathroom to get dressed.

"Lookie what we got here!" a cop cheered when he discovered bricks of cocaine stacked in the closet like shoe boxes. "Bruh, you fucked!"

"That's not mine!" Cortez shouted, setting off a round of laughter. Officer O'Neil came out of the bathroom fully dressed, confusing him even more. "You set me up?"

"Duh, yeah. I'm a cop, dummy!" she laughed. It was known that Cortez was just a middleman but once he saw how much time he was facing he was sure to snitch. Shit rolls uphill too.

"Let me ask you something?" the cop whispered as he escorted the prisoner to a squad car to be transported to the precinct.

"I ain't telling you shit! I ain't no snitch! You won't get me killed! My family killed!" he said loud and proud.

"Nah, chill," he said in a low, conspiratorial tone. "Did you fuck her? Was the pussy good? Man I been tryna fuck her for years!"

*****

"So, how's work?" Megan asked as she and Officer O'Neil did sit ups. Both had rock hard abs as a result of their workout sessions. Both had lovely thighs and fat asses from squats and presses. Both had strong arms that could knock a nigger out if need be.

"It's cool," she said even though the Cortez case left a bad taste in her mouth. Her back up was late busting in the apartment, forcing her to swallow cum. None of the male detectives had to suck dick and drink cum. No, they got to be the cowboys, kicking down doors, guns blazing. She was just bait. A worm never gets the same glory the fisherman gets for catching the big fish.

"Hello?" Megan called with a curious giggle when she saw her friend had drifted away somewhere deep in her own mind. "Are you, OK?"

"No, not really," she admitted but didn't explain. "I'm not sure I can do undercover work. It's, very demanding... "

Megan could only wonder what she meant as she drifted back into her head. Perhaps she could have spared Megan from a similar fate had she explained. She was dead set on following in her dad and now Officer O'Neil's footsteps and become an undercover cop. Seeing the effects of drugs from her project window as well in her own mother made her declare war on drugs.

"I'll be OK though," Officer O'Neil decided and bucked up. "You ready to hit the bag?"

"Always!" Megan cheered. This time it was her turn to hold the bag while Officer O'Neil went first. This time it was her who pounded the bag so hard the gym stopped to take notice. One more bust like Cortez would get her a promotion. He'd given up his connect and it was time for her to connect with him; a love connection that would get her inside his residence.

*****

"What the... " Megan asked when she saw the lump on the log, asleep on the sofa. She cocked her head curiously at her grandmother for explanation.

"Jax let her in. Said she was sleeping in the stairwell," Dianne shrugged as if she didn't know what to do. Megan did though and went for the phone. "Baby?"

"Baby nothing!" she shot back defiantly just as her call was answered. "Yes, you were looking for Michelle Robinson? She's here. Un huh, mmhm, OK."

"What they say?" Dianne asked wide eyed with wonder.

"What you think? They coming to get her! Now take Calvin out somewhere so he don't have to see the stray puppy he brought home get arrested," she instructed. Dianne looked like she wanted to protest but didn't. Instead she collected her grandson to walk over to the park.

Jax gave a long, longing look at the lump on the log as if he knew it would be long time until he saw her again. Megan waited until she watched them walk through the courtyard before waking her mother up. That proved to be easier said than done but she needed to have a word with her before the cops came knocking.

"The fuck?" Megan chuckled when a pitcher of ice water didn't wake her. She dumped it right on her head and the woman didn't budge. "Wow."

Megan shook the suggestion to boil water out of her mind and filled it with tap water. This time she poured it directly into her mouth and nostrils. That made her pop up spitting and sputtering as she almost drowned.

"What the hell is wrong with you?" Michelle asked seriously. She frowned up as if it was Megan out stealing and prostituting for drugs.

"Me? What the hell is wrong with you? How could you do this to yourself? To your family!" Megan pleaded. She was more hurt than mad and powerless to prevent tears from streaming down her face.

"I ain't did shit to myself! Fuck you talking 'bout!" she shot back defiantly. Megan took the mirror from the wall and stuck it in her face while she was ranting. That shut her right up when she saw what she became. She initially flinched at the stranger. Now, it was her turn to shed a tear. Just one since her malnourished body wasn't functioning as it should. "The drugs. They got me fucked up man. I, I, I'on even know what happened. I... "

Megan was stunned when the woman broke down into heavy, heaving sobs, minus the tears. It was that moment of clarity every addict has when they reach rock bottom. Some shrug it off and fall to their death. Some use it as a catalyst and catapult to get their shit together. Michelle got help in her choice when a heavy handed knock on the door interrupted the moment.

"Police, huh?" Michelle asked and nodded knowingly.

"Yeah, ma. It's the police," Megan admitted and went to let them. She let out a sigh and pulled the door open.

"Is Michelle Robin..." the cop said but stopped in mid sentence when he saw her. He obviously saw the anguish and softened his tone. "Time to go, Miss Robinson."

"OK, let me hug my daughter. She gonna be a cop too one day. She gonna be a good cop too. Ain't that right, lil mama?"

"Yeah, ma," Megan said and allowed her the first hug she could remember in life. Her heart broke when she wrapped her arms around the frail woman's emaciated body. She ignored the smell of crack, malt liquor, menthols and semen and squeezed her tightly. "I'ma be a good cop."

"We gotta go," the cop said and gently pulled Michelle's arms behind her back. Megan turned her back as the cuffs were clicked and her mother was taken away. This way Michelle didn't get to see her tears.

Chapter 20

"Look at my baby!" Dianne squealed with delight when Megan stepped out in her cap and gown. She wore a cute pair of capri pants underneath with her shell toed Adidas under them. Fat tears tumbled down the grandmother's face at the sight of her high school graduate.

"Oh stop, grandma," Megan fussed hoping she didn't end up crying too. It was a futile attempt because she was quickly overwhelmed with the accomplishment.

Graduating high school is a given in many suburban neighborhoods, including the one she began her life in. The school she would have attended on Long Island had a 100% graduation rate. The one she attended now had a dismal 32% graduation rate. Some of her peers like Na-Na and Yvonne had children graduating kindergarten today, but wouldn't be graduating themselves. Their only goals now were WIC, Section 8, food stamps and welfare. They would one day get their own project apartments to live in until they died.

"Oh boy," little Jax exclaimed, popping his forehead with his palm. "You two always crying!"

"So what, Bernard!" Dianne cracked and the cracked the family up. As much as she got on Megan about not calling him by his right name, she just couldn't help herself. "My bad, Jax. Now go get dressed so we can watch your sister walk across that stage!"

"OK, grandma," the obedient child agreed and rushed off to comply.

"Let me take this off until we get to the school," Megan said ready to do just that. They had to take a bus and train to school so she didn't want get wrinkled.

"Oh no you don't! Ain't but ten kids from these whole projects graduating today. You gone wear that cap and gown. Stunt on these niggas!" her grandmother insisted.

"Stunt on these niggas?" Megan repeated and shook her head. She could shake it all she wanted because she was going to wear it whether she liked it or not. Once Jax changed clothes and stuffed toys in all pockets they were set to leave.

"See, told you," Dianne said smugly and pursed her lips as they walked through their courtyard. She was right because three more kids proudly wore their cap and gowns on their way to collect a diploma.

"Yeah you told me," she replied offering a fist bump. She saw Na-Na and them on their bench smoking an early morning blunt to get their day started. Nothing much was on their itinerary so the blunt wouldn't hurt.

"OK, that girl Megan 'bout to graduate!" Yvonne cheered genuinely. She and the other girls liked and looked up to Megan. They knew she would be on the news one day and they would all say 'ooh, I knew her!'

"Yeah, thanks," she replied and kept stepping. She had the feeling she would see one or some of them on the news one day and be able to say 'aww man, I knew her'.

Dianne shook her head at the girls for pretty much the same reason. She lived her life long enough to recall their mothers and grandmothers sitting on those same benches decades ago. They would probably leave them to their own children to inherit one day.

Little Jax clowned around the whole way to the high school. The gymnasium was no where near as full as it was for basketball games so there was plenty seats front and center. Megan went to join her fellow graduates back stage and waited for her name to be called.

At her old school it would have taken an hour to reach the letter R for Robinson, but here it only took a few minutes. Megan cheesed widely when she heard her name and came out smiling literally from ear to ear.

"She looks like the joker!" Jax said and cracked up. His grandmother almost popped his leg until she saw he was right. She still snapped some pictures as they were joined by a guest.

"Just made it!" Officer O'Neil gushed as she sat down next to her and began to film with an expensive camera. Dianne frowned curiously at her expensive clothes, shoes, jewelry and purse. Even the perfume she wore smelled expensive and she put a tad bit too much on.

Megan waved and cheered as she joined the ranks of the high school graduates. Some were going to college, others to trade schools or straight to work. She was scheduled to take the police academy test in one week.

Gerald's last name was Williams so he was dead last. His mom had to work and his father was a mystery, so Megan and family cheered him on when he crossed and gave his speech.

"Let me take you guys out to eat!" Officer O'Neil offered once the ceremony ended and Megan joined her family.

"Yes! Burger Hut!" Jax cheered as if the decision was his to make. It wasn't and he was quickly overruled.

"How 'bout no!" Megan shot back. "Let's go to City Island, please!"

"City Island it is! Are you coming Gerald?" she asked. His eyes went wide with shock hearing the question Megan asks when his legs begin to shake during hand jobs. It would be her cue to grab the towel for him to skeet in.

"Oh!" he said a second later when he caught up. He was one of those smart, slow people who took a second to process some things, sometimes. "I don't have extra money right now."

"It's my treat, Mr. Valedictorian! Oh and since you got top honors you get to pick the restaurant," O'Neil offered and smirked at Megan for letting him beat her by a point.

"Where ever she wants to go," he said proving just how smart he really was. A happy girlfriend meant a happy ending later that night. Jacking off is almost like washing a car. You could do it yourself but it's better when someone does it for you.

"Well, let's get to stepping so we can catch this bus," Dianne fussed with the frustration of catching a bus evident in her voice.

"Bus? Please, I'm pushing a brand new Benz," Officer O'Neil huffed and led the way.

Once they were outside she pressed a button on a remote and a shiny four door hollered back.

"Dang! I can't wait 'til I'm on the force and my checks start rolling in. I'ma get me one of these too!" Megan vowed. There's really no such thing as speaking things into existence, unless you're God but it was true. She just didn't know it yet.

Dianne pursed her lips dubiously at the expensive car. She dealt with Officer Johnson long enough to know you don't get a car like that on a cop salary. She, Gerald and Jax got in the backseat for the ride over to City Island and their best seafood in the city.

Dianne pursed her lips again a couple hours later when the bill came. Officer O'Neil didn't bat an eye at the large bill and pulled out an even larger roll of bills from her designer purse. She knew her place and stayed in it which meant staying silent on the ride back to the projects.

"Hole up, Megan. Let me get a quick word with you," Officer O'Neil said once she pulled in front of her building.

"Go on up. I'll be right there," she assured her family and stayed behind. "Sup, chica? We hitting the gym tonight?"

"Nah, I got a... date," she replied ominously. "But check it. This is for you. I'm very proud of you."

"Wow! Thank you," she said accepting a neat stack of cash still in a bank band. Curiosity made her count in on the spot, "A thousand dollars! You must have a rich boyfriend too?"

"Junior's rich alright," she sighed and passed her a set of keys. "This is to my condo. Just hold on to them for me."

"Is everything OK?" Megan dared, squinting and tilting her head to the side.

"Yeah, sure. Catch you later," she said putting the car in gear. Megan caught the hint and reached for the door handle.

"You gonna let me drive this one too?" she asked since the woman taught her to drive in her old Honda.

"Sure," she said dryly and drove off. Megan watched the car bend a few turns until it out of sight. She turned on her heels and headed inside to handle a hand job first chance she got.

*****

"What's wrong, Poppi?" Candy asked, seeing Junior check the rear view mirror for a third time. If someone was following him it wasn't her people since she'd yet to make a case. Once again playing hard to get got her wined and dined by the drug lord. They dated for months before she finally fucked him. She had no choice since he was about to lose interest. Men enjoy the chase, but for only so long before they move on to easier prey and an easier lay. Once she laid some of that good athletic pussy on him he was hooked like a fish. So was she though because his dick game was ridiculous. She would never admit it out loud, but she was beginning to enjoy being loved by the plug.

"Nothing," he said and checked it once more. His demeanor was different lately but even more so tonight. His fist clenched the steering wheel and his jaw was tight.

"We don't have to go out tonight," she offered since she really wanted to go home now. Besides tricking a bunch of money on her, she hadn't seen anything illegal yet. Cortex said he was the man so they sicced her on him.

"It's cool. Got something I wanna show you," he said finally looking at her. He flashed his sexy smile that would have gotten him some pussy even if she weren't undercover. She didn't mind fucking him since he was laying some serious pipe and spending real good. It didn't matter anyway since he was still going to jail. He certainly earned it with all the money he spent on her.

Junior turned up the music to turn down the chatter. Officer O'Neil danced provocatively in their leather seat next to him. She saw him glance at her thighs and took his free hand and put it on it. He could feel the heat emanating from her crotch and slid up her thigh.

"Mmm," she purred when he found her hairless kitty beneath silk panties. She parted her legs a little more to give him room.

"Dang, mama!" he exclaimed at how wet she got at first touch. He was shocked again when she bust all over his fingers. It made his foot heavy and propelled the luxury car towards the Island.

Officer O'Neil paid attention to her surroundings despite busting two more nuts before they reached the secluded house. If this were the main house it would hold evidence more valuable than just drugs and money. This is where the ledgers would be and the overseas accounts, the real money.

"Who lives here, daddy?" she asked cocking her head at the modest house.

"I do. It's my private hideaway. Almost nobody knows where I really live," he explained and got out.

Officer O'Neil pumped her fist at having finally made it to his main house. She was so excited she didn't notice that the usually courteous gentleman didn't open her door. She opened it herself and followed him inside.

"Nice?" she almost questioned the modest digs. Dude was a flamboyant dope boy and didn't do modest. This had to be his main stash spot and the thought of a bust made her pussy wet. So did he since he was a sexy Latino who sucked her vagina like a ripe mango.

"Yeah," he replied in the same stoic manner he'd been using all week. He walked off so she followed hoping they were hopping in bed. They were and ended up in a neat little master bedroom. The furniture all match but looked like it came from a rental store. This was definitely a stash spot and her pussy squished when she walked.

"I gotta get these wet things off," she fussed and sat on the bed. She watched his face go from uninterested to interested in a flash when she leaned back and shimmied out of her panties. She playfully tossed them to him with a giggle. His face turned serious when he saw just how wet they were. He popped them in his mouth and sent a text on his phone.

'Not yet. I'll hit back' he typed and tossed it aside. He then turned the phones camera on her and snapped a few pictures.

"What are you doing?" she giggled and posed. She made a mental note to get his phone when he was arrested and spread her vagina lips to pose them too.

"A little something for my boys in the pen," he said sliding a finger inside of her and taking a picture of that as well. "Jax will love it!"

"Not as much as I do!" she admitted when he replaced his finger with his tongue. She kicked her legs as far open as they would go and lifted her dress over her head. She reached her next orgasm by the time she unhooked her breast. Good pussy is like a good brownie so it was only right he went for seconds.

"My turn," Junior said once he sucked another nut out of her throbbing vagina. She hoped he wanted sex but that hope was dashed when he put his dick in her face.

Having sex with targets was a necessary evil she kept from her boyfriend. It was sucking the dicks that got to her. It was so personal she couldn't kiss her man for weeks. It would be months now when his meat slid in her mouth. She grabbed the thick shaft and tugged it while working her mouth and neck. She had to sigh through her nose since her mouth was full when he snapped a few more pictures.

She was relieved for several reasons when he pulled out of her mouth and laid her on her back. One, because he didn't cum in her mouth and two, because she wanted him inside of her. He took another couple of pictures while working the head of his dick in the froth between her lips.

"For Jax?" she asked even though the name didn't ring a bell.

"Nah, these mmm, for me," he said as he squeezed inside her tight box. He tapped out another text and tossed the phone aside and began to tap on her cervix.

Junior propped up on his hands and looked down to watch himself slide in and out of her. He shook his head when she coated his dick in that good creamy lotion only good pussy produces. He picked up his pace then snatched himself from her snatch and skeeted on her stomach. "Damn, O'Neil, you got some good pussy!"

"Thank y..." she began and paused when she registered him calling her by her real name. Her mind scrambled for an excuse or reason as she looked for her purse containing her gun.

"Told you that pussy good!" Cortez laughed as he entered the room. His presence explained how Junior got her name. She wondered why he was out of jail, but now wasn't the time to discuss it.

"How would you know? All you got to do was eat it," she snapped and reached for her dress.

"Bruh, don't tell me you lied on your dick?" Junior laughed. The look on Cortez's face made him laugh even harder. "You said you fucked the shit out of her!"

"She still a cop!" he shot back since it was all he had. Two more men entered the room killing Officer O'Neil's plan to try the two of them.

"Yeah she still a cop. Now, what you gonna do about it?" Junior asked. On cue one of the men handed Cortez a pistol. He took and looked at it, her, and then him.

"Can we work this out? We can... " O'Neil started to say until Cortez fired at her midsection. She rolled over the bed from the impact but got up ready to fight.

"Uh oh. I think you made her mad!" Junior laughed. Officer O'Neil tried to rush Cortez since he was the one with the gun. He fired twice more and she went down.

"No, please," she pleaded when he walked over and lifted the gun to her face. His was the last face she saw before the lights went out, forever.

"Give that to Jay," Junior said causing Jay to step forward and reach for the gun. "I don't want either of these bodies found."

"Bodies?" Cortez asked looking around for the other one. Jay lifted the gun to the back of his head and fired.

"See, telling me the bitch was a cop after you put her on me really don't make up for putting her on me," Junior leaned down and explained to the corpse. "After I spent all that bread to get you out too?"

"Me da (give me), poppi," Jay interjected so he could get to work. It was a lot of work to break a body down to where it couldn't be found and he was ready to get to it.

"Yeah, yeah. Yo, send her finger to her people. The middle one."

Chapter 21

"Oh man!" Megan groaned when she found what she was looking for in the mailbox. She was so excited she kept it and left the rest in the box. She walked in a slow trance back up the stairs to the apartment. Midway up, the ammonia-like piss smell hit her and she ran the rest of the way.

"Is that it?" Dianne asked with shared enthusiasm. She supported the girl's dream even if she wanted another career path for her. The smart girl could literally be whatever she wanted to be but only wanted to be a cop.

"It is!" she said holding it up like their Olympic torch and dancing from foot to foot.

"Um, where's the rest of the mail?" the grandmother inquired seeing it was all she had with her.

"Huh?" Megan said now remembering shoving the rest back in the box. "I'll go back and get it. You think we should open this?"

"Nah, just sit it on the table," came the silly answer to the silly question. Megan pursed her lips and tore into the envelope. Dianne held her breath as she watched Megan's lips move as she read silently. Her lips spread into another Joker like smile as she passed the letter to her grandmother.

"I scored in the top ten percent, ever!" she cheered despite passing the police test exams to her to read.

"Wow! You gone be chief of police just like you said!" Dianne cheered. She leaned back on the sofa and frowned curiously at a crusty clump on the back. "What the hell is this?"

"What?" she asked and came closer for inspection. Her eyes went wide when she realized what it was. Gerald was a little backed up after not seeing each other for a week. She thought she cleaned up after him skeeting all over the place but missed some. "I'on know?"

"Girl let me find out... " her grandmother warned. After sixty something years on the planet she knew dried cum when she saw some.

*****

Officer O'Neil hadn't taken or returned Megan's calls all day so she brought the test results with her to the gym for their work out session. She figured scoring that high on the exams meant she could pretty much write her own ticket. She decided to skip being a patrol officer like most rookies and jump straight to detective. After a few years of undercover work she would move up to captain, then chief of police.

"Yup, yup!" she cheered along with her plan as she skipped down the street. She had her Joker smile on when she walked into the gym but the somber mood wiped it away.

All she saw was long faces from the police officers that routinely worked out or trained there. She got a sinking feeling when she looked around and didn't see her friend, mentor and big sister, Officer O'Neil. She would usually already be here sweating by the time Megan arrived. She would never be in the locker room but Megan checked there too. She ignored the sad eyes that followed her into the locker room and out. A male officer knew who she was looking for took a deep breath and went to deliver the grim news.

"Where's Officer O'Neil? Must have decided to take a day off. I'll just come back," Megan blurted and tried to leave. The look on his face spoke volumes so she wasn't trying to hear anything he had to say.

"Hey, hold on. Look, what I'm telling you can't be repeated," he began since the murder hadn't been let known to the public. The severed finger was matched to Officer O'Neil and police knew that's all they would be getting. The death notification was made to her parents and arrangements were made to send the finger off in typical, grand, dead cop fashion.

"It's OK. You don't have to tell me anything," she pleaded and tried to leave again. He grabbed her arm to hold her in place and let it out.

"O'Neil's dead. She was undercover and got killed," he said even though it was too much. Too much, yet all they knew. The target was known but anything beyond that was only what Officer O'Neil reported and that wasn't much.

Megan went both numb and deaf upon hearing the news. She frowned at the man speaking, wondering why she couldn't hear anything he was saying. It irritated her enough to pull her arm from his grip and walked away. She was in a daze as she walked back towards the projects. Her name being called was the only thing that made her realize she was back.

"Yo Megan, come chill!" Yvonne called out. She and her friends were always chilling and always invited her to chill with them. She always declined so they were shocked when she changed directions and came over.

"Sup," she greeted stoically and took a seat vacated by a new, young girl.

"Mph," Na-Na said pushing a smoldering blunt towards her while holding smoke in her lungs. They were all shocked when she took it and took a pull.

Megan had watched enough blunts get smoked from her window to know exactly what to do. She took a toke, sipped some air, took another toke and passed on the right hand side.

"OK now!" Yvonne cheered as she took the blunt. Megan followed whoever was talking with her eyes but had nothing to offer to the conversation. It was mainly who fucked who and who had a big dick or big money. She took two and passed when her turn came until the weed was done.

"You got something on the next one?" Na-Na asked. Megan replied by fishing a twenty from her purse. It was her biggest expenditure from the thousand dollars Officer O'Neil gave her a few weeks ago when she graduated.

"I'm out," she announced and stood. She heard them talking to her as she left but none of the words registered. She entered her building and took the pissy steps up by twos.

"Hey, baby. I... "Dianne began but paused when she smelled the freshly smoked weed emanating from the girl. "Baby?"

"Officer O'Neil got killed," she explained and went into the bathroom. She realized just how high she was when she got under the shower. The hot water and euphoria made her as horny as ever. Gerald wasn't here so she slid her own hand between her legs. She came harder and quicker than ever before in her life. Her legs were rubbery and wobbly when she got out to dry off. The munchies set in and sent her into the kitchen. She stood in the open fridge and devoured cold, leftover chicken. Dianne watched her walk back through the living room on her way to bed.

*****

"You ready, baby?" Dianne stuck her head in the door and asked. She saw the girl was fully dressed but that wasn't the question.

"No. I don't want to go," she said frankly. She knew she had to so she lifted herself off the bed. She picked up the keys to the Honda she inherited from Officer O'Neil and followed her grandmother through the house.

"You behave yourself, Jax," Dianne warned from behind a wagging finger since the boy opted to stay home.

"I will," he vowed and it was a 50/50 chance he actually would behave himself. He was a good kid but a kid nonetheless.

"Wish she would have left me the new car," Megan said, surprising them both. She frowned and looked around to see who said that bullshit. The frown on her grandmother's face alerted her that it was she. "I mean..."

"Yeah, I know what you mean baby," she said, knowing people say stupid shit in times of grief and anger. Mainly grief because an angry tongue often times speaks the truth.

Megan pressed her lips tightly to prevent anymore stupid shit from spilling out. A half hour later they arrived at the large church that handled most of their dead cop funerals. Dianne recalled being snubbed at Officer Johnson's funeral when Megan was eagerly admitted. Officer O'Neil listed her as the sibling she never had. She was seated right up front next to her parents. They were all grieving too much for greetings but shared a nod.

No one really listened to the police department preacher preaching her eulogy. They really didn't miss anything since he really didn't know the woman. Megan studied the cops' faces just as she did at her own father's funeral. Most just seemed indifferent, relieved that it was someone else besides them in that box. Only the detectives working the case and the higher ups knew there was only a middle finger inside the closed casket. A beautiful picture of Officer O'Neil in happier times, like alive standing next to the box.

*****

"Go on up. I'll be back in a few," Megan said when they arrived back at the projects. Her grandmother twisted her lips dubiously and stayed put. "You know Carlos has a time limit on being good. You better go check on him."

"Yeah and I'm sure it expired," she agreed and got out to check on her brother. Meagan pulled away the next second after she closed their door. She didn't know the exact address so she drove over to Officer O'Neil's condo from memory. She was always good about taking in her surroundings and if was taken anywhere once she could get there twice.

"Hmp," she huffed seeing the Benz she had been pushing lately. She wished again that it was left to her but kept it to herself this time. She let out a sigh as she used the key to enter the lobby and took a deep breath since it didn't smell like pee. Megan had almost forgot what it was like to not smell urine everyday. It's crazy what people can become accustomed to when not given a choice.

She rode the elevator up to her floor and got out. She remembered to go left to the last apartment and used the key to enter. Her eyes blinked rapidly as they struggled to focus. The last time she was here she had plastic lawn chairs in the living room sitting in front of a 32" TV. Now there was a plush leather sectional that sat in front of a 65" plasma television. The entire unit was laced in leather and chrome.

She ambled around checking out the sights in the unit. A lot had changed since she was last there. Especially the closet, which was stuffed with expensive clothes. More jewelry lay on the dresser and nightstand and it just didn't make sense. A diary on the dresser could not be ignored, so Megan did not ignore it. She picked it up and put it in her purse and left the room.

"Wow, she was dirty?" she surmised with a snarl. She turned her nose up at the trinkets and her friend. Officer O'Neil's words came back and reverberated in her head. *All cops take money. It's part of the job. You will too, watch.*

"Bet you I don't!" Megan fussed and stormed out. She locked the door behind her and dropped the keys in the mail slot.

Chapter 22

"Welcome to the New York City Police Department police academy!" a short, stout man shouted to the class of one hundred men and women. Twenty women were lined up next to the eighty men. "Look to your left. That is your partner for training. One of you will not make it."

Megan looked to her left and saw a prissy Puerto Rican girl. She was pretty and girly with blonde streaks in her curly hair. She wore the same blue training sweat suits everyone else wore but no ones was as tight as hers.

"Hello," they both greeted each other with a smug smile convinced it was the other who was going home early. Megan knew she would make it because she had the knowledge and training and planned to use it. Likewise Marisol knew she had some good, hot Latina pussy and planned to use it.

"Blah, blah, blah," Marisol mocked as the training lieutenant gave his opening day spiel. She thought it was cute but Megan was pissed off. She'd been wanting, waiting and working for this her entire life.

"Chill," she snapped and got snapped on herself.

"Excuse me? Miss... " Lieutenant asked and paused to read her name off her name tag. "Robinson. Am I boring you? Would you like for me to shut up, chill?"

"Sir, no sir," she shot back with her back and eyes straight in perfect attention.

"Good because I have no chill! Nor do I take kindly to insubordination! You may as well not even unpack, Miss Chill," he advised. As he spoke, the rest of the training staff entered the room; the muscular men and women who would carry out the task of training the newest New York Police city officers. "You guys pay particular attention to Miss Chill here. She'll be the first to go."

*****

"Omg, you really pissed Lieutenant off! Why did you tell him to chill while he was talking?" Marisol asked once they reached their shared room. They both headed straight for the bed next to the window and put their bag on it. "You may as well let me get it mama since you gonna be leaving soon."

"Bit... I'm not going anywhere. You can have the bed, but I'm not going anywhere!" Megan vowed.

"Well, we'll see," she said and peeled off her tight sweats. Megan gave her curvy body a curious once over when she reached a matching thong and bra set. Colorful tattoos embellished her pretty tan skin tone and her belly button was pierced. She saw Megan looking and turned, "You like girls too?"

"Huh? No! I," she said getting stuck on an answer. She definitely did not like girls but she liked looking at them. Marisol shrugged and climbed on her bed. "You're not going to study? We have a quiz in the morning." she asked incredulously.

"I need my beauty rest, mama," she replied. Her beauty got her this far in life and she had no plans on using anything else. Now it was Megan's turn to shrug. She sat on her bed and cracked open the manual. She closed it just after 2 AM and went to sleep.

"Rise and shine! Time to grind!" a training officer shouted as he rushed into the room at 5AM . Megan immediately rolled out the bed and hopped to attention. Marisol didn't budge so the instructor rushed and stood over her. "Out the bed! On your feet!"

"Chill, papa," Marisol moaned so seductively Megan turned to look. Just in time to see the young woman open her legs wide to get out of bed. The male instructor's eyes went wide as they shot between her legs. The thin strip of thong wasn't enough to contain the fat vagina underneath. They locked eyes and came to an understanding.

"You two fall out to the wreck yard in five!" he shouted, mainly at Megan. He and Marisol gave another look and nod and he was out.

"Glad he fine," she said getting out of bed. The black man was handsome, chiseled and next in line to get inside that good Latina pussy. She planned on fucking whoever had to be fucked to get through training so it was a plus that he was attractive. A plus, but not mandatory.

Five minutes later, 98 of the hundred were standing at attention on the wreck yard for morning physical training. Two stragglers came running out just as the lieutenant began to speak.

"Good morni... what the heck? You two turn back around and go pack. You're out of here!" he barked at his first two examples of the class. There would be more, they were just first. Most would have to wait a few months until the next class begun. Other would be gungho rent-a-cops at the local mall. "I would have bet you were going to be first, Miss Chill?"

"Sir, no sir!" Megan shot back loud and proud. The lieutenant stifled a proud smile at her conviction. It didn't surprise him since he trained her dad way back when. He was actually taking her under his wing, in his own 'tough love' kind of way.

"Hmp!" he huffed, poking his bottom lip out. Once he finished talking shit he turned the show over to his training officers. They had a five mile run ahead of them, but he was going back to bed.

*****

Five miles later the recruits returned to shower and change. Megan was shocked that Marisol actually finished the run. She just knew Sergeant Williams was going to pick her up and carry her after she showed him some pink. The woman did run track in high school so the five miles were a breeze.

After twenty minutes, they were herded into the chow hall for a hearty breakfast. A heavy meal designed to make the weak sleepy so more examples could be made. Twenty minutes more and they were in class for a quiz on the manual they were given the day before. Megan just knew Marisol was toast now since she went straight to sleep last night instead of reading. And she couldn't flirt with Sergeant Williams to get by since the classroom instructor was a woman.

An early forties, no nonsense black woman who didn't have a dick to cloud her judgment.

"I am Sergeant Hopkins. I will be your class room instructor," she introduced in a monotone cadence.

"I am RoboCop," Marisol snickered. She desperately needed to learn how to whisper because the woman snapped her head in their direction the slander came from.

"Care to repeat yourself?" Sergeant Hopkins dared and cocked her head as she approached Megan.

"Me? I didn't say nothing!" she shouted incredulously. She let out a sigh and shook her head. This girl was going to get her sent home in disgrace. She would end up as a mall cop or a corrections officer.

"I already heard about you, Miss Chill. I got my eye on you." she warned and went back to the front of the class.

The quizzes were passed out and the clock began to run. Megan smiled at the easy questions as she filled in the right answers. Meanwhile Marisol played in her hair and doodled on the paper.

"Time!" the sergeant called in a slightly husky voice and stood. She rushed around collecting the test from recruits still trying to fill out last second questions. She passed out the next manual to be studied for their next test.

Sergeant Hopkins leafed through the test to sort the ones fully completed from the rest. These would be her top recruits. She made a pile of those and sorted the rest into two more piles. Her face contorted when she came to one that didn't contain a single answer.

"Marisol Ruiz?" she called out with a pained expression on her face. Marisol raised one hand while twisting her hair with the other. "Stay after the class is excused. Class excused!"

"Hmp," Megan huffed at the girl as she stood to leave. She was ready to go claim the bed by the window since she was sure she was gone. Instead she went to lunch, then headed to the gym to maintain her physical advantage.

The schedule was clear for a couple of hours so she made the best of it. She was ready to shower and change for more training when she returned to the dorm. She could move her stuff to the other bed too while she was there since it should be empty. Unfortunately the single bed was double occupied when she opened the door.

"What the... " she shrieked seeing Marisol face down, ass up on the bed. She somewhat expected that but didn't expect to see Sergeant Hopkins behind her, eating her out doggy style. She was drunk off that good pussy nectar when she looked up, but didn't stop. Couldn't stop.

"Sss, get it mamacita! Mmm," Marisol fussed and came on her tongue. Megan eased out and closed the door behind her. She knew then she wasn't getting the bed by the window.

*****

The next time Megan found her roommate tooted up doggy style it was Sergeant Williams digging her out. He couldn't stop either when she walked in on them.

"Oh, hey, um Robin-ssson. We um talking about, mmm," he explained as he kept a solid upward thrust into the good, Latina pussy. She could hear it splashing across the room as she eased back out the room.

Each and every, the instructor got to dig Marisol out in exchange for a passing grade. The pussy had to be good because she was atop the list of the remaining 60 students. The lieutenant was the only one who didn't get caught inside the woman. Mainly because he got a blow job in his office. Now came their hand to hand combat part of training. They saved it for the end because it didn't matter how well you did in class or on the range. You still had to have some hands. It was like an MMA, ultimate fighter type of fight where almost anything goes. Kicks, punches and elbows were fair game.

"You will have to go a full round against your training partner!" the instructor announced causing Megan to smile broadly. That good pussy wasn't going to help her in the ring. "It's win or go home!"

It really wasn't a win or go home but the threat made for some good battles. Megan should have known by all the extra male spectators the girls would be first to fight. Two white girls beat each other purple in their first match. It was a good battle even if slightly disappointing since no titty came out. The best thing about a girl fight was the appearance of a stray titty. Sometimes you can get two, three or even four.

"Bout to beat this bitch silly," Megan giggled to herself as she and Marisol got ready on opposite sides of the ring. She pounded the gloves together as her head gear was strapped on by the trainer.

"Be careful," the trainer said as she stood to meet her opponent in the middle of the ring. Megan laughed through her mouthpiece as she and Marisol touched gloves. The bell rung and Marisol swung a back roundhouse kick that almost knocked Megan's headgear clean off.

"You didn't know I was a third degree black belt, huh?" Marisol laughed. Megan was dazed and confused by the hard kick. The crowd of men and Hopkins all cheered and clapped.

Megan got her ass kicked for the next two and a half minutes. It was all she could do to stay upright and stay awake during the three minute match. The problem was that Marisol got smug and kept repeating the same moves. It worked every time and resulted in a punch or kick. Megan memorized the move and waited on it.

"Just go on and quit," Marisol teased and came in. She faked left so Megan would dip right and run dead into another roundhouse. This time Megan dipped left and let the kick sail harmlessly by. The momentum swung Marisol completely around. When she came back around a two shot body blow combination made her spit her mouthpiece out. She saw the uppercut speeding into her life but had no way to stop it.

"Shit!" the lieutenant laughed when the blow lifted Marisol off her feet. She was asleep in midair and snoring when she landed. The bell rang and Marisol was declared the winner. The ref raised her hand while she slept on the mat. "Ain't this some shit..."

*****

"And there's the Joker!" little Jax teased when he saw his big sister standing on the stage with her fellow police academy graduates. Teasing aside he beamed with pride. All of his friends sisters had babies or sexually transmitted diseases while his was now a New York City police officer.

"Shut up, Horatio," Dianne cracked up. Her grandson twisted his lips and shook his head. Even he thought it was funny now but would never admit it.

"That's my girl!" Gerald said and sighed. He missed her and her hands during the two month training. He certainly could have jacked his own dick but where's the fun in that.

The ceremony was as full of pomp as a police funeral. Most didn't catch the similarities but Megan did. As happy as she was she still felt a sense of dread. She just knew she would one day be the guest of honor lying in box covered by a flag. All she could hope was that she didn't have her picture beside a closed casket. It's really bad when you're so fucked up they have to close the lid.

"We did it, chica!" Marisol cheered and hugged her neck. "I didn't think you was going to make it!"

"Yeah, well," Megan replied and left the rest unsaid. The hug she returned was truly genuine. She actually learned a lesson from the slut. She would modify it slightly since the promise of pussy is just as potent as parting with the pink.

Once the ceremony was over the rookies were given their assignments. Megan just knew she would hit the streets and rid the world of crime. She guessed Marisol would be stuck behind a desk so the higher ups could go higher up inside of her.

"Ruiz. 44th precinct, patrol." the lieutenant read from his assignments. "Robinson. 13th precinct, intake desk."

He saw her reaction to his assignment and waited for the rest to clear before approaching her.

"Lieutenant, why am I in Manhattan riding a desk while err'body else gets to work the street? I'm a cop, not secretary!" she fussed.

"Intake was the only slot open down at the 13th," he expanded which only explained half his reasoning.

"Then put me in another precinct!" she said stomping her foot like a girl. She caught herself and tried again. "Why the 13th?"

"Because that's where your father worked."

Epilogue

"Mmm," Jax moaned watching a stunning blow job in process on the screen of a phone. She would periodically pull his dick out and lick the length like an ice pop then pop it back into her mouth. He moved the phone and looked down so he could see it directly.

"Mmm," the female guard hummed when his legs began to rock. She threw her neck into overdrive sensing he was about to lose it. She clamped down and braced herself for the impending explosion.

"Shit! Fuck! Mmm," he fussed and moaned as he skeeted down her throat. He rocked her head back and forth to milk himself dry. Once the spams subsided he let her up.

"You straight? Need anything else?" she asked eager to please both him and Junior. The only reason the young woman got the job was to take care of Jax's needs. Today he needed his dick sucked and shrimp scampi for lunch.

Jax did an easy bid with most of the comforts of home.

"I'm good," he said just as his phone began to ring. He smiled at the number and took the call. "Sup, yo?"

"You, my dude. How you holding up?" Junior asked. "Did you get what I sent you?"

"Yeah, she's here now. I like this one better than the last one."

"Well don't knock this one up and she can ride the rest of the way. About halfway done, huh?" he asked. Junior tried to pay his way out just like he did for Cortez but had no luck. Jax was a bad cop who killed a good cop and got away with it. He was going to do his whole time.

"Little more. I doubt they fucking with me on parole," he said watching the shapely ass leave his cell.

"No worries, papa. I got you. And when you get home you gonna be right beside me. My number two guy!" Junior assured him.

"That's what's up. Me and you, homie," Jax said with far more enthusiasm than he felt. They said their goodbyes and terminated the call. Jax could only shake his head and laugh.

"Number two. Nobody wants to be number two."

To Be Continued